This book belongs to

Elise Kimmich

Bluebell Glade

Dandelion Dell

Heart of Misty Wo[od]

Hawthorn Hedgerows

Fairy Animals

of Misty Wood

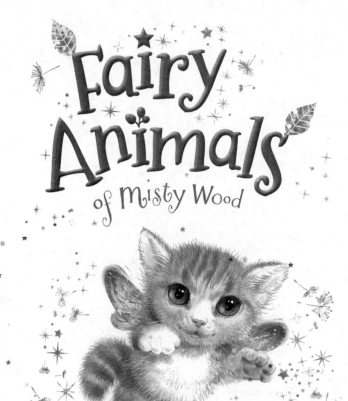

Kylie the Kitten

Lily Small

Henry Holt and Company
New York

With special thanks to Anne Marie Ryan

Henry Holt and Company, *Publishers since 1866*
Henry Holt® is a registered trademark of Macmillan Publishing Group, LLC.
175 Fifth Avenue, New York, NY 10010
mackids.com

First published in the United States in 2017 by Henry Holt and Company.
Originally published in Great Britain in 2014 by Egmont UK Limited.

Library of Congress Cataloging-in-Publication Data
Names: Small, Lily, author.
Title: Kylie the kitten / Lily Small.
New York : Henry Holt and Company, 2017. |
Series: Fairy animals of Misty Wood ; [book 9] | First published in 2014 by
Hothouse Fiction Ltd. | Summary: Kylie's excitement over going to summer camp
with her friends is threatened by her fear of the water. Includes activities.
Identifiers: LCCN 2017028189 (print) | LCCN 2016057766 (ebook) |
ISBN 978-1-250-29718-1 (Paper Over Board)
Subjects: | CYAC: Fairies—Fiction. | Cats—Fiction. | Animals—Infancy—Fiction. |
Camps—Fiction. | Fear—Fiction.
Classification: LCC PZ7.S6385 (print) | LCC PZ7.S6385 Kyl 2017 (ebook) |
DDC [Fic]—dc23
LC record available at https://lccn.loc.gov/2017028189

Our books may be purchased in bulk for promotional, educational, or business use.
Please contact your local bookseller or the Macmillan Corporate
and Premium Sales Department at (800) 221-7945 ext. 5442
or by e-mail at MacmillanSpecialMarkets@macmillan.com.

First American edition, 2017
Printed in the United States of America by
LSC Communications, Harrisonburg, Virginia

1 3 5 7 9 10 8 6 4 2

Contents

Chapter One
Camp Sunshine 1

Chapter Two
Acorn Team 20

Chapter Three
Woodland Treasure Hunt 41

Chapter Four
Showtime 64

Chapter Five
Morning Glory 85

Chapter Six
The Boat Race 108

CHAPTER ONE

Camp Sunshine

It was dawn in Misty Wood.
The sun was just starting to rise,
painting the sky with beautiful
stripes of rosy pink and purple.

Kylie the Kitten lay on her mossy bed, listening to birds chirping in the fir tree overhead. Their sweet songs usually woke Kylie up, but today she was awake long before the birds started to sing.

Kylie jumped out of bed and arched her back, stretching her glittering blue-and-golden wings.

She glanced at her reflection in a little pool of dew. Then she licked her velvety paws and smoothed down her fluffy white-and-ginger fur. Kylie wanted to look her very best today.

"Good morning," Mom purred from the other side of their home in the roots of the fir tree. "Would you

like a honey-and-berry muffin?"

Honey-and-berry muffins were Kylie's favorite breakfast, but this morning she was too excited to eat. It felt like she had a family of butterflies inside her tummy! Kylie nibbled a few bites, and then brushed the crumbs off her whiskers. Padding over to a toadstool, she picked up a little basket resting on top. It was made from woven flower stems.

4

Most mornings, Kylie used her basket to collect water from Dewdrop Spring. Like all the fairy animals of Misty Wood, Kylie had a very special job to do. Cobweb Kittens like Kylie decorated the cobwebs of Misty Wood with dewdrops so they sparkled in the morning light. But today Kylie was using her basket for something else. She was packing for summer camp!

5

Every year, the older fairy animal children were invited to spend a weekend at Camp Sunshine. It was the first time Kylie was old enough to go! She'd heard lots about camp from the other Cobweb Kittens. There were teams and challenges and prizes to win. It sounded like so much fun—and best of all, her friends Connie and Chloe were going, too!

Kylie had never spent the

night away from home before. She
suddenly worried that she might
feel homesick at bedtime. Then
she had an idea. She went outside
and fluttered her wings, heading
from tree to tree until she spotted
what she was looking for. Stretched
between two branches of a tree was
a lacy spiderweb. Kylie carefully
took the web down and folded it
neatly. Now she had something to
remind her of home.

"It's almost time to go!" Kylie's mom called up to her.

Kylie fluttered back to where her mother was waiting.

"Do you have any space left in your basket?" Mom asked.

Kylie nodded, holding it up.

Mom popped a few muffins into the basket and twitched her tail playfully. "I know you're too excited to eat now, but you might get hungry later on."

It was finally time to head out.
Kylie and her mom fluttered their
wings and rose into the air.

Below them, Misty Wood
stretched out like a glorious paint

9

palette, its colors shining in the morning light. Everywhere they passed, fairy animals were busy working to make the wood a beautiful place to live.

In Honeydew Meadow, Bud Bunnies were hopping into the sunlight, ready to nudge open the buds of the yellow buttercups. Nearby in the Heart of Misty Wood, Bark Badgers were carving beautiful designs on the tree trunks.

Holly Hamsters were nibbling patterns into holly leaves, and Moss Mice were shaping mossy cushions with their paws.

As they flew over Dewdrop Spring, Kylie could see the Cobweb Kittens filling their baskets. They laughed as they dived in and out of the glittering fountain, catching dewdrops that twinkled like diamonds.

The grown-up Cobweb Kittens

waved to Kylie and called, "Have fun at camp!"

Kylie waved back, but she flew higher in the air to avoid the dazzling jets of water. Although Kylie loved making cobwebs sparkle, she wasn't very fond of getting splashed. You see, Kylie had a secret. It was such a big secret that not even her very best friends knew about it. She was scared of water!

Kylie and her mom flew a bit farther, past a little waterfall and over a glade of trees, and then Kylie's mom said, "Here we are!"

Just ahead of them was Moonshine Pond, shimmering with pearly light. Lily pads dappled the water's surface, and long, fuzzy cattails and pretty blue irises grew all around the pond.

"But this is Moonshine Pond," Kylie said, confused. From the

14

name, she'd guessed that Camp
Sunshine was in a sunny meadow.
Oh, dear—this wasn't very good
at all.

"The camp is just there, by
the bank," said Mom. She pointed
toward a row of colorful tents
tucked back from the water's edge.

As Kylie got closer, she saw
that the tents were woven from
reeds, and each one was decorated
with a different flower. Glossy red

15

poppies, bright yellow daffodils, pretty bluebells, and snowy-white lilies all sweetly perfumed the air.

The camp looked lovely, but Kylie felt scared. What if water from the pond splashed her? Or even worse—what if the campers had to go swimming?

"Actually, I think I'd rather stay home," she fretted.

"Don't be silly," her mom said. "You'll have a brilliant time."

16

As Kylie and her mom
landed on the banks of the pond,
young fairy animals were playing
everywhere. Two Pollen Puppies
were wrestling on the ground, while
a fluffy Bud Bunny played tag
with a group of tiny Moss Mice.
A small cluster of Dream Deer
and Hedgerow Hedgehogs stood
giggling together.

Kylie looked around nervously,
but she couldn't see her Cobweb

Kitten friends anywhere. Everyone else seemed to have made new friends already.

She gulped. First there was the pond, and now Kylie was on her own. The butterflies in her tummy returned, but this time they were flying loop-the-loops!

CHAPTER TWO

Acorn Team

A beautiful, pale yellow Petal
Pony trotted over to Kylie, her
shimmering blue wings open wide.
"Welcome to Camp Sunshine!"
she said. "Is it your first time here?"

Kylie nodded shyly.

"I'm Poppy," the pony said, flicking her silky mane out of her kind eyes. "I came to Camp Sunshine last summer and had so much fun. You're going to love it here! Come and meet everyone."

Kylie looked over at the other fairy animals nervously. Would anyone want to be her friend?

"Are you feeling shy?" Poppy asked her gently.

"A little bit," Kylie admitted.

The pony smiled at Kylie. "That's just how I used to feel," she said. "Not too long ago, I was much too shy to talk to anyone."

But Poppy seemed so friendly and brave. "What did you do?" Kylie asked.

"I learned that if you're kind, everyone will want to be your friend," Poppy said. "And camp is a great place to make new friends."

22

Kylie suddenly felt much better. If Poppy could make new friends, then so could she!

Kylie turned to her mom. "I'll miss you," she meowed, burying her face in her mom's ginger fur.

23

Mom nuzzled Kylie's nose and said, "I know you'll have a wonderful time, my brave girl." Then she fluttered her wings and set off for home.

Kylie and Poppy flew over to the crowd of campers, who had begun to form a circle. Two Stardust Squirrels were also arriving, their bushy tails leaving a shimmering trail of stardust behind them.

"Hurry up, Sally," the older

squirrel called to the younger one, who was scurrying after her. Then she squealed, "Hi, Poppy! Come and sit next to me." She turned to her younger sister. "Stay here, Sally. I'm going to play with my friends."

The squirrel named Sally sat down next to Kylie. A Bud Bunny with soft white fur and spots the color of chestnuts hopped over and sat down on Kylie's other side. Her

25

whiskers were trembling, which made Kylie think that she might be feeling a bit nervous, too.

Plucking up all her courage, Kylie said, "Hello. I'm Kylie. Is this your first time at Camp Sunshine?"

The Bud Bunny nodded. "I'm Bonnie." Then she added in a whisper, "I was so nervous about coming here that I couldn't eat any clover this morning!"

Kylie smiled and held out her

basket. "Would you like a honey-and-berry muffin?"

Bonnie took one and started nibbling. Her purple eyes lit up. "Yummy scrummy in my tummy!"

Kylie giggled. She liked Bonnie. Her mom and Poppy were right—it was easy to make new friends when you were kind! Kylie asked the Stardust Squirrel on her other side if she'd like a muffin, too.

"Thanks," the squirrel said,

helping herself. "I'm Sally. My
big sister Suzy came to camp
last summer, so I can tell you
everything you need to know."

But before Kylie and Bonnie

28

could ask her any questions, a
Bark Badger made his way into
the middle of the circle and held
up a strong black paw for silence.
The campers stopped chattering
and listened with respect, for Bark
Badgers were very kind and wise.

"Welcome to Camp Sunshine,"
the Bark Badger said. "I'm Barry,
the camp leader. We have a very
exciting weekend planned for you."

He smiled kindly at the

campers. "But first, let's sing our welcome song. Can the campers who've been here before help me teach the others?"

"Oooh—I know this song already," Sally whispered to Kylie and Bonnie. "My sister taught me."

Barry cleared his throat and began to sing in a deep voice. Poppy, Suzy, and the other older campers chimed in loudly, and before long everyone else joined in.

"We love it at Camp Sunshine
Where the days are long and fine.
We have fun in the summer sun,
Welcome, welcome, everyone!"

When they'd finished singing, Barry said, "Over the next two days you'll be working in teams."

I hope I'm on the same team as Connie or Chloe, thought Kylie, waving to her Cobweb Kitten friends. She'd finally spotted them sitting across the circle.

31

"This weekend is all about making *new* friends," continued Barry. "So we've put you all on teams with different fairy animals."

Excited chatter broke out. Then Barry picked up a piece of bark carved with names and read out the teams. Poppy the Petal Pony was on Pinecone Team. Chloe was put on Chestnut Team, and Connie on Buttercup Team. More teams were called, but Kylie wasn't on

any of them. Had the Bark Badger

forgotten her?

"And last but not least, we

have Acorn Team," Barry said.

"Petey, Bonnie, Sally, and Kylie."

Kylie and Bonnie looked at each other in delight. They were on the same team! Kylie's tail twitched happily, and Bonnie hopped with excitement.

A brown puppy bounded over and somersaulted to a halt in front of them. Scrambling onto his white paws, he gave a cheerful salute and barked, "Petey the Pollen Puppy reporting for Acorn Team duty!"

Sally the Stardust Squirrel

fluffed out her tail. "The first thing we need to do is pick our tents," she said. "Follow me, girls!"

Kylie and Bonnie scampered after her toward the tents.

"How about this one?" Bonnie suggested, pointing at a tent with delicate sprigs of lavender.

"No, this one's much better," said Sally, hopping over to a tent covered with garlands of bright orange lilies. Without waiting for a

reply from the others, she pushed through the ferns that made the tent's door flap.

Kylie and Bonnie followed her inside. As she looked around, Kylie gasped. The beds were mossy cushions, just like hers at home. But these cushions were stacked on a frame made out of sticks—one on top of the other!

"I'll have this one!" cried Sally, fluttering up to the highest cushion

36

and wrapping her fluffy tail

around her like a blanket.

Kylie chose the bottom bed.

She padded over and set down

her basket. Then she took out her

cobweb and spread it carefully over her moss cushion.

"What's that?" Sally asked, looking down and frowning.

"It's a cobweb," explained Kylie. "To remind me of home."

"I think it's pretty," Bonnie said.

"We don't need a boring old cobweb to make this tent pretty!" cried Sally. "I've got a much better idea." She leaped down from the top bed and spun around in circles. Her

CHAPTER THREE

Woodland Treasure Hunt

Kylie and her teammates scampered outside. Along with Petey, who was sharing a tent with a Dream Deer

and a Hedgerow Hedgehog, Acorn
Team made their way to Barry.

"The first fun activity is a
Woodland Treasure Hunt," he told
the campers. "It's a great test of
speed and teamwork. Each team
must find five different woodland
treasures. The first team to return
with all five will be the winner."

Barry handed Kylie a piece of
bark with their instructions. Petey,
Bonnie, and Sally huddled around.

42

"We need to find an oak leaf and a twig," Kylie said, pointing at the beautiful pictures Barry had carved with his sharp claws.

"Ooh! And some moss and a daisy," Bonnie said.

"And a big stone, too," Petey added.

Kylie was relieved that they didn't have to bring back any dewdrops from Dewdrop Spring.

"Easy peasy summer breezy,"

43

Sally said. "I know where to find all those things!"

Kylie glanced at the other teams, who were studying their lists and murmuring quietly. "Maybe we should make a plan first," she suggested shyly.

But Sally was too busy jumping up and down and cheering. "We are Acorn Team, so shake your furry tail! We are Acorn Team and we will never fail!"

Petey's tail wagged so fast
it looked like a blur! Bonnie was
hopping up and down, too.

Then Barry clapped his
hands and called, "Have fun and
remember to work together." He
tooted loudly on a reed flute and
the Woodland Treasure hunt began!

"Shall I get my basket?" Kylie
asked the others. "It might be
handy for carrying our treasures."

"There's no time for that,"

cried Sally. "Let's go!" She opened

her wings and flew up into the air.

Petey and Bonnie followed after her,

their wings sparkling like rainbows.

Not wanting to be left behind,

Kylie beat her wings as quickly as she could. "Where should we go first?" she asked breathlessly.

"To the Heart of Misty Wood, of course," ordered Sally. "That's where I gather acorns. There are lots of oak trees there."

The midday sun warmed their backs as they flew to the very center of Misty Wood. Trees spread out beneath them like a sea of green. Kylie and her new friends

47

fluttered down to the ground. It was much cooler here, deep in the woods. The leaves overhead rustled in the breeze.

"This is lovely," Petey panted, rolling around on the soft ground.

"We don't have time to play," said Sally bossily. "We need to find an oak leaf."

"I see one!" cried Bonnie, hopping over to a big tree. She came back waving a green leaf.

"Yippee!" called Kylie. "We've got the first treasure on our list!"

Petey ran into the woods for a moment, and came back with a twig in his mouth. He dropped it at their feet with a flourish. "Here's the second treasure!"

"Hooray!" Kylie and Bonnie cried together.

"I've spotted something, too," Sally said. She scampered over to the oak tree's trunk, where its thick,

49

twisty roots grew out of the damp soil. She scooped something up in her paws, and came back holding a velvety pile of moss. "That's the third thing," she said proudly.

"So what's next?" Petey asked.

Kylie checked. "A daisy."

"I know where there are lots of daisies," the Pollen Puppy yelped. "Just follow me!"

Team Acorn rose into the air again. As they flew over Moonshine

Pond, Kylie glimpsed the row of colorful tents. None of the other teams had returned yet.

"Hurry, team!" cried Sally.

The Golden Meadow stretched in front of them, its green grass dotted with yellow buttercups and dandelions.

Petey dived down and tumbled into a bed of dandelion clocks, scattering fluffy white seeds everywhere. "Whee!"

The long green grass tickled Kylie's tummy as she landed on the meadow. Nearby, a group of Pollen Puppies were frolicking, wagging their tails and sending up clouds and clouds of fluffy pollen so that new flowers could grow.

"Hi, everyone!" Petey called to the Pollen Puppies. "Have you seen any daisies?"

A white Pollen Puppy with a black patch over one eye pointed

across the meadow. "Try over there,
just past that patch of clover."

Kylie and the others dashed
across the meadow after Petey,
whose long ears streamed out

behind him. Then he came to a sudden stop and they all tumbled over him into the grass.

"Oops-a-daisy," joked Petey.

Kylie stood up, laughing. They were surrounded by green stalks topped with small, round buds.

"Oh no," Petey said, his laughter turning to dismay. "The daisies haven't bloomed yet."

Oh, dear, thought Kylie, biting her lip. Sally looked *very* annoyed.

54

"I'm sorry," whimpered Petey.
"I really thought we'd find a daisy
here."

"You've forgotten that there's
a Bud Bunny on your team," Bonnie
reminded him. Hopping over to the
daisy buds, she nudged them gently
with her twitching nose.

"Ta-da!" she said. As if by
magic, the buds started to unfold,
one white petal at a time. Then
the flowers lifted their yellow faces

up to the sun and bobbed joyfully in the breeze.

"Wow!" Kylie breathed.

"It's just what we Bud Bunnies do," Bonnie said modestly. Then she picked a daisy and tucked it behind her long, silky ear. "What's the last treasure we need to find?"

"A big stone," Kylie replied.

Everyone thought hard. Where, oh where, could they find a big stone?

"I've got it!" cried Kylie. "There are lots of big stones around Crystal Cave."

"That's not far from here," said Petey. With a flurry of beating wings, the fairy animals flew toward the Crystal Cave. Soon Kylie could see the crystals inside twinkling like fairy lights.

"Kylie was right!" shouted Petey. "There are lots of big stones."

The fairy animals landed just

57

outside the cave. Grunting with effort, Petey picked up a big stone. "If you take the twig, Kylie, I'll carry this."

But when Petey fluttered his wings, nothing happened. He tried again, beating his wings harder. Still he stayed on the ground.

"What's wrong?" Sally asked, frowning.

"The stone's too heavy," Petey gasped. "I can't fly with it."

58

"Let me try," Sally said. "I'm very strong." She picked up the stone and fluttered her wings—but it weighed her down, too.

"If only we'd brought Kylie's basket along," Bonnie said sadly. "We could all help carry it."

That gave Kylie an idea. Without stopping to explain, she dashed into Crystal Cave. It was dark and spooky inside. Kylie felt along the rough walls until she

found something soft and silky.
Gathering it up, she ran back
toward the sunlight.

"A cobweb?" said Sally rudely,
when she saw what Kylie was
holding. "How's that going to help?"

"Cobwebs look delicate, but
they're actually very strong," Kylie
explained. She spread the cobweb
on the ground and placed the stone
right in the middle. Then she laid
the leaf, the twig, and the moss next

to it. "If we each take one corner of the web, we should be able to fly our treasures back to camp."

Everyone picked up a corner. "On my count," Kylie said. "One . . . two . . . THREE!"

The fairy animals fluttered their wings furiously and rose into the air, lifting the cobweb along with them.

Kylie held her breath. Would the cobweb hold?

It sagged in the middle, but the web held strong as they flew with their treasures back to Camp Sunshine. They landed on the banks of the pond and then sprawled on the ground, panting.

"Well done, Acorn Team," said Barry as he came over to greet them. "What a clever way to carry your treasures."

"Did we win?" Sally asked him breathlessly.

"I'm afraid not," Barry said kindly. He nodded at the pond, where Suzy, Connie, and two other fairy animals were splashing in the water. Team Buttercup had won the treasure hunt!

CHAPTER FOUR
Showtime

"I expect you're hot after all that hard work," Barry said, seeing the disappointment on Acorn Team's faces. "So why don't you cool

off with a nice dip in Moonshine Pond?"

"Come for a swim, Sally," her sister called. "The water's lovely!"

"Time for a doggy paddle!" barked Petey, bounding toward the pond.

"Last one in is a stinky toadstool!" Sally cried, chasing after him. Soon most of the campers were splashing in the water. But Kylie hung back.

65

"Don't you want to go swimming?" Bonnie asked her.

Kylie didn't want to tell Bonnie her secret. Her new friend seemed kind, but Kylie was afraid she'd laugh. It was silly for a Cobweb Kitten to be scared of water!

Kylie looked over at the other

campers playing in the pond. Sally
and her sister were floating on their
backs, their tails spread underneath
them like fluffy rafts. Poppy the
Petal Pony was letting a little Moss
Mouse and a Holly Hamster slide
down her long neck and splash
into the water. Petey was clowning

around, wearing a lily pad on his head. Everyone was having so much fun. But even the thought of dipping her paw in the water made the butterflies in Kylie's tummy come back.

"Er . . . my tummy hurts a bit," Kylie said.

"You poor thing!" Bonnie exclaimed. "I'll keep you company."

Kylie and Bonnie stretched out under a weeping willow tree. They

68

gazed up at the blue sky dotted with clouds as white and fluffy as Bonnie's tail.

"Why don't we look for pictures in the clouds?" Bonnie suggested. She pointed her paw up at the sky. "See! There's a fish."

Kylie tilted her head and squinted at the cloud. It *did* look like a fish. What a fun game! She stared up at the sky and suddenly saw lots of interesting shapes. "Ooh!

69

That one looks like a pinecone.

And that one looks like a hedgehog

balancing on a toadstool."

The rest of the afternoon flew

by. When the sun had dipped lower

in the sky, Barry called the campers

over for their dinner.

Kylie's eyes grew wide when

she saw the feast laid out on a big

old tree stump. There was wild

mushroom medley, watercress

salad, a big pile of hazelnuts, and

heaps of plump, juicy blackberries.

It all looked wonderful!

Kylie and Bonnie filled their

acorn bowls to the brim and sat

down with Petey and Sally around

a toadstool table. Mmm—it tasted delicious! Kylie finished every bite of her dinner, and still had room for a big bowl of blackberries.

A full moon shimmered overhead. Stars twinkled against a velvet sky and fireflies swirled through the night air like sparklers. Owls hooted softly and crickets chirped, singing Misty Wood to sleep with their lullabies. But the campers weren't ready for bed yet.

"Now for our next activity! We're going to put on a talent show," Barry said. "Each team will work on an act, and the team that gets the loudest applause will win."

Acorn Team huddled together.

"I can dance!" said Bonnie.

"And I can juggle," Petey said, picking up three hazelnuts and starting to juggle them.

Sally plucked the hazelnuts out of the air and popped them in her

73

mouth. "I've got a better idea," she said. "We'll put on a play."

"What will it be about?" asked Kylie.

Sally thought for a moment. "It will be about a beautiful and clever Stardust Squirrel who dances in the moonlight. I will play the Stardust Squirrel, of course."

"Who will the rest of us be?" asked Bonnie, disappointed.

"Hmm," said Sally. "Kylie and

Bonnie, you two can be trees. And Petey, you can be . . . the moon."

They started practicing their play. Sally told everyone where to stand and what to do. Then, as Sally pranced about and said her lines, Kylie and Bonnie waved branches in the air, pretending to be trees. Kylie swayed and tried to look treelike, but wished she had a bigger part.

Petey was supposed to stand

still and look serious, but he kept humming a lively tune and chasing his tail. *"Clap your paws and make a sound,"* Petey sang under his breath. *"Find a partner and spin them around."*

"Stop it, Petey!" Sally said crossly. "We won't win if you don't do what I tell you."

"But it's boring," whined Petey. "You're the only one who gets to do anything interesting."

"Maybe we should try

something different," suggested
Bonnie.

"Like what?" asked Sally,
sulking.

"I know!" said Kylie. "We can
all perform Petey's song together."

Even Sally had to agree it
was a good idea. They had just
enough time for a quick rehearsal
before Barry called everyone back
together. It was showtime!

Chestnut Team was the first

to perform. They had written a
sweet poem about Camp Sunshine
and recited it together. After that,
Buttercup Team did a comedy
routine, with every team member
telling a funny joke. Kylie laughed
so hard that her sides ached.

Pinecone Team was on next.
They did a breathtaking flying
display, turning loop-the-loops
and zooming around upside down.
For their finale, they all flew in

a perfect V-shaped formation
with Poppy the Petal Pony at the
center. Kylie thought she looked
beautiful, as her blue wings
glittered in the moonlight and her
silky tail fluttered in the breeze.
When Pinecone Team finished with
dramatic nosedives to the ground,
the applause was deafening.

After a few more acts, it was
finally Acorn Team's turn. Kylie
squeezed Bonnie's paw for good

luck as they nervously waited for
the music to begin.

Petey started them off, beating
out a rhythm on an acorn drum.
Then Sally joined in, playing a
lively tune on reed pipes. Kylie and
Bonnie danced in time to the music
as they all sang Petey's song:

"Clap your paws and make a sound,
Find a partner and spin them around.
All the fairy animals sing along now—
Doo-bee-doo, then BOW-WOW-WOW!"

80

Kylie and Bonnie whirled
around faster and faster. Every
time it came to the chorus, they
bowed to each other and spun
around the opposite way. The

81

audience clapped along happily to the music.

When the song was over, Acorn Team bowed and basked in the applause. Kylie could see her friends Connie and Chloe cheering loudly. The crowd had clearly enjoyed their act, but was it enough to win?

Kylie held her breath as Barry read out the results.

"It was close," he said. "Acorn

Team's song got a very loud cheer, but the winner of the talent show is . . . Pinecone Team!"

"Oh, conkers and cobwebs," muttered Sally. "Second again."

Kylie shrugged and smiled at her team. "I still had fun."

As Poppy and her team proudly took another bow, a pale figure drifted overhead, casting a long shadow over the performers.

Kylie glanced up. "What's

that?" she asked, pointing at the spooky shape.

"I don't know," Bonnie whispered nervously.

"Eek!" shrieked Sally. "It's a ghost!"

CHAPTER FIVE

Morning Glory

Kylie gasped as the spooky figure
hovered in the air. Could it really
be a ghost? She and Bonnie and
Sally clung to one another in fright.

But then Suzy laughed. "Don't be so silly," she said. "It's just a Moonbeam Mole."

Kylie peeked past Bonnie and saw a Moonbeam Mole flying over the pond. He tipped out his net and scattered glittering moonbeams over the water. They bobbed on the surface, making gleaming, pearly ripples. It was lovely!

The campers called hello to the Moonbeam Mole, who gave them

a friendly wave in return. Then he

flew away again, his silvery wings

twinkling.

"If the Moonbeam Moles have woken up and started their work, it must be time for us to go to bed," Barry said. "Come on, kids."

"But I'm not even sleepy!" Petey protested with a stretch and a big yawn.

As the pond's dark water shimmered in the moonlight, Kylie headed back to the tent with Bonnie and Sally. Her new friends fluttered to their beds, and Kylie curled up

on her mossy cushion, snuggling under her cobweb blanket.

"Nighty-night," Sally called softly from the top bed.

"Sleep tight," whispered Bonnie from the middle bed.

But Kylie fell fast asleep before she could even reply.

Kylie was having a lovely dream about dancing under a starry sky with a Moonbeam Mole. They were

scattering moonbeams all over Misty Wood, twirling faster and faster until—

"Wakey, wakey, sleepyhead," called Sally. "Time to rise and shine."

Kylie opened her eyes and looked around the tent. Where was she? Then she smiled. It was her second day at Camp Sunshine!

Kylie licked her paws and quickly washed her face. Then she

and the girls stepped out of their tent into the glorious early-morning sunshine. They joined the other campers for a tasty breakfast of seedy loaf and rosehip jam washed down with cups of acorn milk.

"I hope you all slept well," Barry said with a smile. "Today each team will be making something very special."

"I wonder what it will be," Bonnie said.

"I bet we'll be weaving baskets," Petey guessed. "Or maybe Barry will teach us wood carving. You can make a picture of me if you like!" He stood on his hind legs, wagged his tail, and stuck out his long pink tongue.

Kylie and Bonnie giggled. Petey was *so* funny!

"Don't be silly," Sally said, rolling her eyes. "We're camping, so I'm sure we'll be making tents.

My sister went here *last* year, remember."

But Sally and Petey were both wrong. After breakfast, Barry gathered the campers by the side of Moonshine Pond. "Today you'll be making boats," he revealed with a smile.

"Yay!" shouted Petey. "I've always wanted to go sailing!" He danced a wild sailor's jig.

But Kylie suddenly felt very

93

cold. Oh no! She definitely did *not* want to go sailing!

To her relief, Barry explained that they wouldn't be sailing the boats themselves. "Each team will make a model boat, and at the end of the day you'll race them on the pond," he said.

Kylie let out a breath. She could be brave enough to go *near* the pond, as long as she didn't have to go *on* it!

"Right, let's get started," said Sally, rubbing her paws together. "Acorn Team has *got* to win today!"

"Maybe we should plan our boat first," Kylie said. She picked up a twig and started sketching a boat in the thick, oozy mud at the edge of the pond.

"That's a waste of time," Sally said impatiently. "I already know how to make a boat. Come on!"

"Aye, aye, captain," Petey said,

and the rest of the team followed the trail of sparkling stardust from Sally's tail. Kylie followed, too, but Sally's bossiness *was* starting to annoy her a bit.

Sally led her teammates to a grove of trees. "Find as many sticks as you can," she ordered them.

Bonnie and Kylie scampered to and fro, gathering up twigs in their paws. Petey dragged bigger sticks over in his mouth.

96

Soon there was a big pile by
Sally's feet. She started to weave
the sticks and twigs together into
the shape of a boat. The others

tried to help, but Sally shooed them away. "Fetch me some nice long grass," she said.

"Fetch this, fetch that," Petey grumbled as they plucked the longest blades of grass they could find.

"I thought puppies liked to play fetch," Kylie joked, but secretly she was glad she wasn't the only one who thought Sally was being bossy.

When they returned with the grass, Sally used it to tie the twigs together. Kylie looked on, wishing she could help.

"There! It's done," Sally announced, sounding pleased with herself. "Now let's test it out."

Kylie and her team carried the boat back to Moonshine Pond. It was surprisingly heavy.

With a big heave, Sally pushed the boat into the water. But instead

of sailing away, it just bobbed on
the surface.

"Why isn't it moving?" Sally
muttered.

"Er, it *is* moving, Sally," Petey
said. "Just not the way we want
it to."

They looked on in horror. The
boat was slowly sinking into the
pond! Down, down, down it went,
until finally it vanished underwater.
A few bubbles floated to the

surface and then—*pop!*—they were gone, too.

"Oh no!" Sally wailed.

"Don't worry," Bonnie said, giving Sally a hug. "We have plenty of time to make another boat."

"And we'll *all* help," Kylie said, smiling at Petey.

This time, Acorn Team sat by the pond and planned their boat before they started building it.

"The way Sally tied the twigs

101

together was very smart," said Kylie.

"But maybe it should be lighter," suggested Bonnie.

They all gathered more twigs. This time Sally collected lots, too, and they soon had plenty. Everyone helped to build the boat, trying out different designs until they decided on the best shape.

"I've got an idea," Petey said. He splashed into the pond and

paddled over to a cluster of lily pads. Petey put the lily pad on his head and swam back to shore with it flopping into his eyes.

Is Petey being silly again? Kylie wondered.

Sloshing out of the water, Petey carefully pressed the big, round lily pad into the boat. "This will be a waterproof lining," he explained.

"Clever!" Kylie said, helping to smooth it down.

"Now we need a mast," said Bonnie.

Petey dragged a long stick over, and Sally tied it to the middle of the boat. Bonnie picked a morning glory vine and wound it around the mast. Twitching her nose against the vine, she nudged its flowers open until the mast was wreathed in blue blossoms.

But the boat still needed a sail. Kylie had an idea. "I'll be right back!"

She quickly flew to her tent and scooped up her lacy cobweb. Then she flew back to the boat and carefully tied it to the mast. There were still drops of water glistening on the lily pad lining, so Kylie sprinkled them onto the sail as a finishing touch.

Then she and the others stepped back to admire their boat. It was sleek but sturdy. The lacy cobweb sail billowed gently in

the breeze, and the drops of water twinkled like crystals in the sunshine.

"It's beautiful!" breathed Kylie.

"Let's go test it out," Petey suggested.

But it was too late. The other teams had all gathered around Barry. The race was about to begin!

CHAPTER SIX

The Boat Race

Acorn Team carefully carried their beautiful boat to the pond. A light breeze ruffled the sparkling water. It was a perfect day for a boat race!

The other teams' boats were
wonderful. Poppy's Pinecone Team
had obviously been inspired by
their name. They'd built their boat
from fir cones glued together with
sticky pine sap.

Chestnut Team had made
their boat from silvery birch bark.
Its green sail was a quilt of leaves,
daintily stitched together with
grass.

Buttercup Team's boat had

the most unusual design. Two
small logs floated on the water,
and a raft made from sticks rested
between them.

Still, Kylie thought that Acorn

Team's was the most beautiful by

far. She crossed her paws for luck.

Barry licked his paw and held

it up to see which way the wind was blowing. "Ahoy there, campers! On my signal, you'll launch your ships." He pointed his paw to the bank of the pond beneath the willow tree. "The first boat to land on the other side of the pond will be the winner."

The teams readied their boats. Petey tinkered with the lining, and Kylie made sure the cobweb sail was still firmly attached. The

112

cobweb was as light as a feather,
but Team Acorn knew how strong it
really was.

"We've just got to win," Sally
said. She shook her tail and gave the
boat a sprinkling of stardust for luck.

Kylie hoped the lucky stardust
would work—and that their boat
wouldn't sink this time. If only they'd
been able to test it. . . .

"Anchors aweigh!" cried Barry,
and the race was on!

Bonnie, Petey, and Sally waded into the pond, but Kylie hung back. She didn't want to get too close to the water. She watched anxiously as her friends gave the boat a gentle push.

The beautiful boat bobbed in place for a moment. Kylie held her breath. Would it float?

Yes! It sailed away, gliding over the rippling water, and quickly took the lead.

"Yay!" Sally cried. "Let's go to the finish line so we can watch it win!"

Kylie hesitated. What if the boat got into trouble and they weren't there to help? "Shouldn't we wait a bit?" she said.

"Don't be such a worrywart," Sally said. "Come on, we don't want to miss the finish!"

Sally took off across Moonshine Pond. Bonnie and Petey flitted after her. All around Kylie, excited fairy

animals were making their way to the other side.

Kylie was about to follow when she noticed that their boat had tilted to the side and changed its course. It was heading straight toward a patch of reeds!

"Wait!" she cried, but the others were already off.

Kylie watched in horror as their lovely boat sailed right into the reeds. Soon it was hopelessly

tangled in the long, marshy grasses.

In the distance, Kylie could see Bonnie, Sally, and Petey heading to the finish line. But their boat would never get there if it stayed stuck! Kylie knew she couldn't let that happen.

Gathering all her courage, she opened her wings and rose into the air. She flew to the patch of reeds and hovered over the boat.

Fluttering her wings furiously so that she wouldn't fall in the water, Kylie reached down and gave the boat a nudge, but it didn't move. She pushed it again, harder this time, trying not to get wet. Still the boat was stuck fast.

By now the other boats were already halfway across the pond.

"Help!" Kylie cried. "Acorn Team!" But all the fairy animals were at the other side of the

118

pond, and their cheers drowned out Kylie's desperate cries.

Kylie thought about her teammates waiting for the boat that would never get there. They had worked so hard and this was their last chance to win a prize at Camp Sunshine. As the boat struggled to break free of the reeds, Kylie's heart sank.

There was only one thing to do—but was she brave enough?

She took a big gulp of air and squeezed her eyes shut. She *could* do it. She had to.

Then she dived into the water!

A moment later, she came spluttering to the surface, her eyes opened wide with surprise. The water felt slippery and . . . *lovely*! Moving the reeds out of the way, she gave the boat a big push, and it sailed free.

Kylie paddled her paws until

she reached the side of the pond.
Then, after clambering out, she
flew over to the finish line.

"Why are you all wet?" Bonnie
asked.

121

"Our boat got tangled in some reeds," Kylie said. "But I got it out."

Their boat was moving swiftly across the pond now, its cobweb sail blowing in the wind. It had nearly caught up to the other boats.

"Come on, little boat!" cheered Bonnie.

It cruised past Buttercup Team's boat.

"You can do it!" shrieked Sally.

It glided past Pinecone Team's boat.

"Almost there!" barked Petey.

But Chestnut Team's boat was just too far ahead. It cruised to the finish line first. Chestnut Team cheered and hugged each other. Moments later, Acorn Team's boat reached the finish line, in second place once again.

"I'm so sorry," Sally said, her voice trembling. "I should have

listened to you, Kylie. If we'd all
been there to help you, we might
have gotten the boat free sooner
and won." Tears glistened in her

eyes. "I was being bossy again. Just like my big sister always bosses *me* around."

"It's okay," Kylie said, giving her a hug. "We still did really well. You should be proud that we finished second!"

"If it wasn't for your quick thinking, we wouldn't have finished at all." Sally sniffled.

When all the boats had finished, Barry gathered the

125

campers for the end-of-camp prize-giving ceremony. "Have you all had fun?" he asked the campers.

Kylie and the other campers shouted, "Yes!" and cheered loudly.

First, Barry presented Buttercup Team with the Treasure Hunt award. On a piece of bark he'd carved a beautiful picture of a treasure chest. As Suzy went up with her team to collect the award, Sally cheered the loudest. But Kylie

could tell how badly her friend had wanted a prize, too.

"Don't worry," she reassured Sally, patting her fluffy back. "There's always next summer."

Pinecone Team was given an award carved with stars for winning the Talent Show. Poppy trotted up with the other members of Pinecone Team on her back to collect their prize.

Finally, Chestnut Team

bounded up to receive their prize, which was carved with a picture of a boat. Kylie clapped her paws together and cheered for all the winners. It would have been nice to win something, but Kylie was just happy to be there. She could hardly believe it was nearly time to go home.

But to her surprise, Barry held up another award.

"And now, for a very special

128

prize," he announced. "The Camp Sunshine Team Spirit award goes to four of our newest campers. Over the past two days, this team has learned how to work together—even when it wasn't easy. Most important, they've become good friends and that's what Camp Sunshine is all about! Congratulations . . . Acorn Team!"

Sally leaped up and down, sprinkling glitter from her tail in

129

excitement. Petey ran around in circles, and Kylie hugged Bonnie tight. Then they all went up to collect a beautiful bark award carved with a smiling sun and a row of tents.

As the other campers cheered, Kylie glowed with pride. Coming to Camp Sunshine was the best thing ever! Not only had she and her new friends won an award, but she wasn't scared of water anymore.

She'd never have to worry about Dewdrop Spring again.

Kylie sighed happily. It was the perfect ending to a perfect weekend. Camp Sunshine was even better than she'd dreamed it would be. She'd made so many friends and had so much fun. Kylie couldn't wait to come back next summer!

Spot the Difference

The picture on the opposite page is slightly different from this one. Can you circle all the differences?

Hint: There are eight differences in this picture!

Camp Sunshine Word Search

Can you find all
these words from
Kylie's story?

ACORN   COBWEB   TEAM   POND   CAMP   TREASURE
DAISY   SONG   BOAT   LILY PAD

A	C	O	B	W	E	B	B	P	C	T	E	A	M	D
E	A	D	A	I	S	Y	S	O	N	G	F	H	E	B
A	M	B	D	A	C	O	R	N	E	R	A	E	A	O
O	P	L	I	L	Y	P	A	D	N	O	P	T	E	A
D	A	I	M	P	T	R	E	A	S	U	R	E	I	T

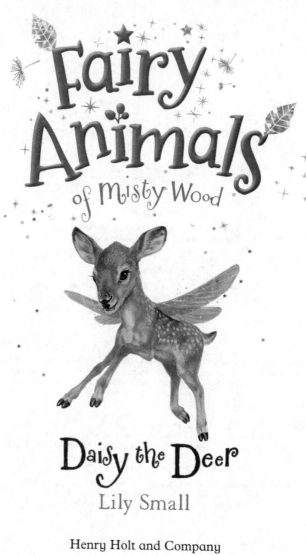

Fairy Animals
of Misty Wood

Daisy the Deer

Lily Small

Henry Holt and Company
New York

With special thanks to Susannah Leigh

Henry Holt and Company
Publishers since 1866
175 Fifth Avenue
New York, NY 10010
mackids.com

First published in the United States in 2017 by Henry Holt and Company.
Originally published in Great Britain in 2014 by Egmont UK Limited.

Library of Congress Cataloging-in-Publication Data

Names: Small, Lily, author.
Title: Daisy the deer / Lily Small.
Description: New York : Henry Holt and Company, 2017 | Series: Fairy animals
of Misty Wood | Summary: Daisy the Dream Deer loves flying around in the moonlight,
whispering happy dreams into the ears of the sleeping fairy animals, but when she comes
across a little hedgehog who is too scared to sleep, can Daisy persuade him that there is
nothing to be afraid of in Misty Wood?
Identifiers: LCCN 2016020539 (print) | LCCN 2016046483 (ebook) |
ISBN 978-1-250-29718-1 (Paper Over Board)
Subjects: | CYAC: Fairies—Fiction. | Deer—Fiction. | Hedgehogs—Fiction. | Animals—
Fiction. | Dreams—Fiction. | Fear of the dark—Fiction. | Bedtime—Fiction.
Classification: LCC PZ7.S6385 Dai 2014 (print) | LCC PZ7.S6385 (ebook) | DDC
[Fic]—dc23
LC record available at https://lccn.loc.gov/2016020539

Our books may be purchased in bulk for promotional, educational, or business use.
Please contact your local bookseller or the Macmillan Corporate
and Premium Sales Department at (800) 221-7945 ext. 5442
or by e-mail at MacmillanSpecialMarkets@macmillan.com.

First American Edition—2017
Printed in the United States of America by LSC Communications, Harrisonburg, Virginia

1 3 5 7 9 10 8 6 4 2

Contents

Chapter One
Sweet Dreams, Misty Wood   1

Chapter Two
The Hedgehog Gobbler   24

Chapter Three
The Night Fright   43

Chapter Four
The Lost Moonbeams   64

Chapter Five
A Special Visitor   81

Chapter Six
The Best Dream Ever   105

CHAPTER ONE

Sweet Dreams, Misty Wood

It had been a beautiful day in

Misty Wood, and now the sun was

ready to go to sleep. As the sky

1

turned from bright blue to deepest purple, the stars began to twinkle and the moon climbed to join them. Down below, the Bud Bunnies were curled up in their cozy burrows, the Pollen Puppies' tails had stopped wagging, and the Cobweb Kittens snoozed in their mossy beds.

But not *everyone* was asleep.
Oh no. Some fairy animals were
just waking up! They were sniffing
the cool evening air, fluttering their
wings, and thinking about their
special jobs, which made Misty
Wood such a wonderful place to
live.

On the banks of Moonshine
Pond, the Moonbeam Moles had
already popped out of their tunnels
and were bustling about gathering
their nets. Soon, they'd all be busy
collecting moonbeams to drop into
the pond so that it would glisten
and shine.

Over on Sundown Hill, a
Dream Deer called Daisy was
stretching her long, slender legs.
She blinked her big brown eyes,

4

smoothed her pale blue fur, and
flexed her silvery wings. Daisy's
special job was to fly around the
wood at night, delivering wonderful
dreams to the sleeping fairy
animals.

"I think I have the best job
of *all*!" Daisy sighed happily. She
bounded to the top of Sundown
Hill and gazed at Misty Wood.
Usually it was very quiet at night,
but tonight the wind was rushing

5

around, making the grass whisper and the trees rustle. Leaves whirled this way and that. But Daisy didn't mind. She spread her wings and the breeze caught them, lifting her into the air.

"Wheeeee!" she cried as a gust blew her toward Golden Meadow. "It's going to be fun, flying in the wind tonight!"

She landed lightly at the edge of Golden Meadow, where the

flowers ended and the trees began.
"Time to start work!" she said.

She trotted slowly along a little
pathway that snaked between the
trees, looking out for any sleeping
fairy animals. It wasn't long before
she caught sight of some little white
whiskers and cute pointy ears,
tucked into a cozy nook in a tree
trunk.

"I know those ears," Daisy
whispered with a smile.

They belonged to Connie the
Cobweb Kitten, one of Daisy's
friends. Connie was fast asleep.
Daisy tiptoed closer, then poked her
soft nose into Connie's snug, warm
home. The little kitten would receive
Daisy's first dream of the night!

"You've just left Dewdrop
Spring, where you collected a big
basket of dewdrops," whispered
Daisy in the kitten's velvety ear.
"There are enough to hang on *all*

9

the cobwebs in Misty Wood, to
make them sparkle and shine! And
then you see a big bowl of fresh
cream."

Connie's button nose twitched

in her sleep, and she gave a tiny, happy meow.

"It looks delicious," Daisy went on, "but you're not sure if it's for you. Then you see a name on the bowl—*CONNIE*. It *is* for you!"

Connie licked her lips with her little pink tongue, and she began to purr. Daisy smiled and crept away, knowing that Connie would enjoy her bowl of cream for the whole night.

11

Daisy leaped elegantly into the air and let the wind carry her toward Moonshine Pond. Above the water, the Moonbeam Moles flitted back and forth, catching moonbeams in their nets. Daisy couldn't be sure, but they looked as though they were working doubly hard tonight.

She spotted a pretty mole with rich purple fur and silver-gray wings.

"Yoo-hoo, Maddy!" she called, cantering along the bank.

Maddy was Daisy's best friend. Sometimes, when they'd both finished their work for the night, they would go off together to play in the meadows. It was lovely to share the moonlight with a friend when all the other animals were asleep.

Maddy swooped and landed next to Daisy, waving her net.

13

"Hello, Daisy!" she said, sounding a bit out of breath. "I'm really sorry, but I can't stop and chat tonight."

Daisy glanced up at all the moles whipping to and fro in the wind. "Why? What's going on? You all look so busy."

"Yes," said Maddy, her dark eyes shining. "We're having a competition. And you'll never guess—the first prize is a yummy

14

dessert. A big brambleberry crumble!"

"Ooooh," Daisy gasped, her mouth watering. "Brambleberry crumble's my favorite!"

Maddy smiled. "Mine too!"

"So, what do you have to do for your competition?" asked Daisy.

"The first mole to collect one hundred moonbeams wins," Maddy explained.

"One hundred? That's loads!"

15

Daisy exclaimed. "Do you think
you can do it?"

Maddy peered into her net.
"I'm doing *quite* well," she said.

16

"I've already got about twenty. I'd
better keep going because I really,
really want to win."

"Yes, of course." Daisy nodded.
"I'll come back to see you later.
Good luck!"

Daisy watched as Maddy took
off, whizzing after a moonbeam
with her net. She soon caught it,
and Daisy grinned. Maddy had a
good chance of winning—she was
so determined. All the same, Daisy

felt glad she didn't have such an energetic job to do. Hers was much more peaceful. She opened her wings and flew off toward Heather Hill, where she was sure she'd find plenty of sleeping animals to whisper dreams to.

At the foot of the hill stood some old oak trees. Their twisting roots made lots of nooks and crannies that were perfect for fairy animals to sleep in. As Daisy drew closer, she

spotted a small bundle curled up on some leaves. She floated down to see who it might be.

"A Hedgerow Hedgehog!" she exclaimed to herself as she landed beside him. "Now, I wonder what sort of dream he'd like?"

She thought for a moment, then bent down to whisper in the little hedgehog's ear. But just as she was about to begin, he jumped up, his prickles spiking

out in all directions. Daisy leaped
back quickly, before a spike could
hurt her nose. The hedgehog
started running around in circles,
flapping his russet-red wings.

"Hey," Daisy called. "I thought
you were asleep!"

The hedgehog stopped running
and looked up at her with sad,
fearful eyes. "No," he said. "I
wasn't. I'm awake."

"I can see that," said Daisy.

"But you're a hedgehog, and hedgehogs aren't supposed to stay up all night! You must be so tired from tidying up leaves all day. I was just about to give you a lovely dream."

The hedgehog's bottom lip began to quiver. "I don't want a dream," he said in a wobbly voice.

Daisy stared at him. "But everyone *loves* dreams."

The hedgehog shook his head.

DAISY THE DEER

"Well, I don't. And I don't want to sleep." He stamped his tiny foot. "In fact, I'm never going to sleep. Never, ever, EVER again!"

23

CHAPTER TWO

The Hedgehog Gobbler

"Never?" Daisy's big brown eyes opened wide.

"No, never!" the hedgehog cried. He curled up in a ball and

began to sob. "And you can't make me!" came his muffled voice.

"It's okay," Daisy said softly. "Don't worry. I won't try to make you sleep. But will you tell me your name?"

"I'm H-H-Herbie," the hedgehog stammered.

"Hello, Herbie. I'm Daisy." She sat down beside him. "So, why don't you want to sleep?"

A fat tear rolled down Herbie's

25

cheek. "Because of the Hedgehog Gobbler."

Daisy stared at him in astonishment. "The . . . what?"

"The Hedgehog Gobbler!" cried Herbie. "He's a horrible monster that comes and gobbles up hedgehogs while they sleep! He creeps up from behind, and then he opens his big mouth with its rows of jaggedy teeth and . . . *chomp!* He gobbles you up."

Daisy frowned. "I've never heard of a Hedgehog Gobbler before."

"Well, he's around here somewhere," Herbie said, peering

over his shoulder. "He could pounce at any time. That's why I'm going to stay awake forever from now on. I'm never going to go to sleep and let him catch me!"

Daisy tried to remember all the different creatures that she knew lived in Misty Wood. There were Moss Mice and Bud Bunnies and Petal Ponies and Pollen Puppies. Cobweb Kittens, Moonbeam Moles, and Stardust Squirrels . . .

28

but she had never, ever heard of a Hedgehog Gobbler.

"I really don't believe there's such a thing as a Hedgehog Gobbler," she told Herbie in a gentle voice. "I think you should try to get to sleep, and then I'll give you a lovely dream that will help you forget all about it."

"But there *is*!" Herbie insisted. "So I *can't* sleep!" His bright eyes filled with tears again.

"All right, Herbie," Daisy said hurriedly. "But you're going to get awfully tired."

The hedgehog wiped away his tears with his tiny pink paw. "I won't get tired." He fluttered his wings and flew in a circle. "I'm wide awake—see?"

Daisy sighed. She could see that Herbie had made up his mind. But perhaps if he got *really* tired, he'd have to fall sleep. And she

knew she could definitely help him there. . . .

"Well, I have an idea," she told him. "If you're going to stay awake, how about you help me with my job?"

"What, delivering dreams?" Herbie asked, looking a bit more cheerful.

"That's right," said Daisy. "If you come with me, you'll have to fly around all night, so the Hedgehog Gobbler won't be able to find you."

Herbie started to grin. "Wow. I'd love to," he said. "I think you have an amazing job!"

"Well, yes, I do like it." Daisy smiled. "Come on, then. Let's head for Honeydew Meadow first."

They took off in a whirl of leaves. Herbie whooped with glee and chased after them. Daisy was pleased. The more energy the little hedgehog used up, the better. They dipped and dived, riding the breeze

33

and enjoying the feel of the wind buffeting them to and fro.

When they reached the meadow, Daisy pointed down at a moss cushion surrounded with flowers, their buds shut tight for the night. On top of the cushion lay a Pollen Puppy, sound asleep.

"We'll start here," she told Herbie as they landed next to the puppy.

"So, what do we do?" Herbie

asked, his eyes shining with excitement.

"We'll think of all the things that a Pollen Puppy loves," she explained. "Then we'll whisper them into his ear."

"Ooooh. Well, I know they love juicy bones to chew," Herbie said eagerly. "And they love chasing one anothers' tails and scampering around the meadows flicking pollen and having fun."

Daisy nodded. "That's great, thank you," she said. "Now I can make a lovely dream for him."

She bent forward and began to murmur into the puppy's floppy ear. "You're having a wonderful time chasing your best friend's tail in Honeydew Meadow . . ." she began.

The Pollen Puppy's paws twitched, and his tail thumped against his mossy cushion.

"Look at him!" squeaked Herbie. "He's really enjoying it!"

Daisy smiled and carried on. "You're bounding past a horse chestnut tree when all of a sudden you spot a delicious bone. . . ."

The puppy gave a happy whine, and his ears pricked up in his sleep.

"The bone is big and juicy, so there's plenty for you to share," Daisy whispered. "You and your

37

friend have a lovely time, eating it and playing with it together!"

The puppy rolled over onto his back and wriggled in delight, his paws waving in the air. Daisy stepped back, proud of their work.

"That was fantastic!" Herbie exclaimed as they slipped away. "Can we do another one?"

Daisy grinned at him. "Of course!" she said. "Come on, let's go into the Heart of Misty Wood. Lots of fairy animals will be asleep in there."

They glided toward the center of the wood, then swooped down between the trees and began to flutter along near the ground,

watching for sleeping creatures.
Herbie was clearly enjoying every
minute, but he seemed to be getting
sleepy, too. His flying was getting
slower, and he gave a great big
yawn. Daisy slowed down as well,
feeling pleased. Her plan was
working! Soon Herbie would be so
tired he'd have to stop for a rest.
Then, when he'd dropped off, she'd
give him the best dream ever.

But suddenly Herbie cried out.

"Daisy!" he shouted. "Stop! Stop! It's the Hedgehog Gobbler!"

"What? Where?" Daisy whirled around in a circle.

"THERE!" Herbie pointed behind her with a trembling paw.

41

Daisy turned and gasped. Right ahead was an enormous towering figure. It was making an awful groaning sound—and it had HUGE waving arms!

CHAPTER THREE

The Night Fright

Daisy gulped. "Hide behind me,"
she said to Herbie, sounding a lot
braver than she felt.

Herbie didn't need to be told

twice. He quickly scuttled behind Daisy.

Daisy took a deep breath and faced the figure. "Who are you?" she demanded.

"I told you—it's the Hedgehog Gobbler!" squealed Herbie.

Daisy tried to stay calm. *There's no such thing as a Hedgehog Gobbler*, she told herself firmly. Plucking up her courage, she took a step toward the huge creature.

"Careful, Daisy!" whimpered Herbie. "I know you're a deer, but it might get you, too!"

"Don't you worry, Herbie," Daisy told him. She peered forward to get a better look . . . then she sighed with relief. "It's not the Hedgehog Gobbler," she said, looking down at Herbie.

"It's not?" Herbie whispered.

Daisy smiled. "No. It isn't a monster at all. It's a tree!"

45

"What do you mean, a tree?"
Herbie huffed, sticking out his
prickles. "It can't be. It's got arms!"

"There's nothing here to
hurt you," Daisy assured him. "I
promise. Come on. Come and see."

Herbie peeked around Daisy's
legs. Sure enough, all that stood
before them was a big old beech
tree. Its trunk was shadowy in the
moonlight. The "arms" were its
branches waving wildly in the wind,

THE NIGHT FRIGHT

47

and the groaning sound was just its roots creaking.

Herbie's prickles began to calm down. "Oh yes," he said happily. "Silly me. It *is* just a tree."

He scampered forward and skipped all the way around the trunk, clapping his wings together as he went. Daisy sighed. At least Herbie felt safe again, for now—but the trouble was, being frightened by the tree had really woken him

48

up. Now he didn't look the least bit sleepy.

"Let's go somewhere else, Herbie," Daisy suggested. "I think the trees look a bit too scary in the moonlight. We'll go to Hawthorn Hedgerows instead."

"Good idea," said Herbie, fluttering along next to her. "Lots of Moss Mice sleep there."

"Will you help me find one?" Daisy asked.

49

Herbie puffed out his chest proudly. "Of course."

Sure enough, it didn't take Herbie very long to find a tiny Moss Mouse curled up in a cozy nest of twigs and moss.

"Well done," said Daisy. "You're being a big help. Now, let's think. What do Moss Mice like?"

"Poppy seeds," Herbie said at once. "And hawthorn berries. I think they like *my* favorite food,

too—yummy hazelnuts. And they love being all together, having fun with their families and friends."

Daisy nodded. "Thank you. That's plenty to work with." She bent down to make a perfect dream for the mouse.

"It's your birthday," Daisy whispered into his tiny ear.

The mouse's nose and whiskers twitched in excitement.

"All your friends are here, and

51

your whole family, too," Daisy continued. "Everyone's having a lovely time. Your mom has made a delicious hawthorn-berry pie, and there's hazelnut cake for later."

"Yum!" Herbie exclaimed, rubbing his tummy. "Make sure they all sing a song," he added. "I love it when fairy animals sing songs at parties."

Daisy smiled and nodded. "Everyone eats piles of poppy seed pancakes," she whispered to the mouse. "Then they all sing 'Happy Birthday' to you. It's your best birthday party ever!"

They watched as the mouse

gave a little squeak of happiness
in his sleep, and then they tiptoed
away. Another good job done!

Daisy led Herbie to Dandelion
Dell, where the flower heads were
closed up for the night. The stems
were rocking to and fro in the
breeze. "Are you tired yet?" she
asked the little hedgehog. She was
quite sure that he must be by now.

"Not a bit," said Herbie.
"I'm getting hungry, though.

And thirsty." He looked at Daisy hopefully. "Where do you think we should go next?"

Daisy sighed. How was she ever going to get Herbie to sleep?

"Let's go to Moonshine Pond," she said. "You can have a drink there. And maybe we'll find a snack on the way."

As they started flapping their wings, a big gust of wind whisked them both up into the air. Herbie

55

did a loop-the-loop as the breeze
lifted him.

"Wheeeee!" he yelled as he
zoomed past Daisy, upside down.

Daisy dived after him,
laughing, then chased him all the
way across the meadows and dells.
As they swung around a clump
of bushes, she spotted something
dangling in the moonlight.

"Herbie!" she called. "Come
back here!"

Herbie did a somersault in the air to turn around.

"You said you were hungry, didn't you?" asked Daisy.

"Yes, I'm starving!" Herbie said, zooming up.

"And I think you said that you love hazelnuts?"

"Ooooh, yes," Herbie cried. "They're my favorite. Why, have you found some?"

"A whole bush of them,"

said Daisy. "And they're just ripe enough to eat!"

Quickly, they gathered a little pile of nuts, and Daisy helped Herbie crack them open with a stamp of her hoof. Herbie chomped his way through half of them, and then stopped.

"I'm full now," he sighed, rubbing his tummy. "But I could really use a drink."

"No problem," Daisy said,

launching herself into the air again.

"We're not far from the pond now."

Above Moonshine Pond, the
Moonbeam Moles were still hard
at work, gathering moonbeams as

fast as they could. While Herbie swooped down to the banks of the pond to slurp the crystal-clear water, Daisy looked around for her friend Maddy. She flew over the pond, weaving in and out of all the busy moles, but there was no sign of her.

"That's strange," muttered Daisy. "Where has Maddy gone? Surely she's still here catching moonbeams?"

And then, just as Herbie flew up to join her again, she spotted Maddy—all alone on the banks of the pond, standing by a clump of bullrushes.

"There's my friend," she told Herbie. "Let's go and talk to her!"

As they fluttered down to land beside Maddy, Daisy's heart gave a little thud. She could tell right away that something was wrong. Maddy was looking very gloomy. Her

silver-gray wings were drooping
and her velvety fur looked flat.

"Maddy, what's wrong?" asked
Daisy.

Maddy gave a loud sniff.
"There's been a disaster," she said
in a trembly voice. "A *total* disaster,
in fact!"

CHAPTER FOUR

The Lost Moonbeams

"A disaster!" Daisy exclaimed. "What's happened?" Then she noticed something was missing. "Maddy, where's your net?"

"That's the disaster," said Maddy, a tear trickling down her nose. "I was just chasing a lovely big moonbeam when the wind came along and blew my net away—*whoooosh!*"

"Oh no!" Daisy felt so sorry for her friend. Maddy had been working really hard.

"It was nearly full, too." Maddy sat down and buried her face in her paws.

"But that's not so bad, is it?"

Herbie asked, looking puzzled.

"Can't you get another net?"

Maddy gave a little sob. "Yes,

but—but not tonight. Not in time to

win the competition." She quickly
explained the rules to Herbie.
"And I was so close! I almost had
a hundred moonbeams and now
they're all lost!" A tear rolled down
her face, and she wiped it way with
her paw.

"Oh, Maddy, please don't cry.
We'll help you look for it," Daisy
said kindly. "It can't have gone too
far. Herbie here will help, won't
you, Herbie?"

"Of course I will." Herbie gave a little skip of excitement. "I love hunting for things. Hide-and-seek is my most favorite game ever."

Maddy peeked at them from between her paws. She was looking a teeny bit hopeful now. "Would you?" she asked.

"Yes! Come on, let's go—there's no time to lose!" cried Daisy.

Herbie was already up in the air with his wings spread, riding

68

circles on the wind. "Let's look in trees first!" he yelled.

He shot off at full speed with Daisy and Maddy just behind. The branches of the trees were swinging, their leaves jostling and rustling, but there was no sign of Maddy's net. So they flew on toward some small bushes on the other side of Moonshine Pond. Herbie dived under them and whizzed over them, but there was still no sign of the net.

"Now where can we look?"
wailed Maddy. "I'll never find it.
And I'll never win the contest and
get my brambleberry crumble!"

But then Herbie glanced up.
"What's that?" he cried, his prickles
on end. He looked at Daisy, his
eyes wide with fear. "Is it—is it—the
Hedgehog Gobbler?"

Daisy followed his gaze and
gasped. There was something
very strange among the stars! A

71

mysterious glowing light, traveling quickly across the sky.

"No, no, no, that's not the Hedgehog Gobbler," she reassured him.

"Yes, it is," Herbie said, flying around in fright. "Those are his big scary eyes, glowing at us."

"I told you, there's no such thing as the Hedgehog Gobbler," Daisy said firmly. "Shall we go and see what it really is?"

"Only if you go first," Herbie said fearfully.

"Okay, come on, then!" Daisy called. She launched off with Maddy and Herbie on her tail.

Up, up, up they flew, over the trees and high above the Heart of Misty Wood. The glowing object was still ahead of them, whirling and dancing in the wind. Daisy beat her wings even harder, until finally she got close enough to see

73

what it was. And when she did, she couldn't believe her eyes!

"Maddy, it's your net!" she called. "It's glowing because it's so full of moonbeams!"

Daisy rushed after it, but Maddy and Herbie were struggling to keep up. Their little wings were whirring, and they were out of breath already!

"Please . . . can . . . you . . . catch it . . . Daisy?" Maddy gasped. "Your wings . . . are bigger . . . than ours."

74

"I'll do my best!" Daisy cried.

She surged forward after the net. The wind whipped through her pale blue fur and made her brown eyes water, but she tucked her head down and flew faster, faster, faster—faster than she'd ever flown before! Maddy's net spun and twisted through the air, turning cartwheels as it shot over the dark trees of the wood. Daisy swished this way and that, following the net

75

as it flew above the treetops and headed toward Dewdrop Spring.

Daisy beat her wings even faster. Now she was close enough to see all the different moonbeams glistening inside the net. She hoped none of them had fallen out.

"One more push!" she said to herself.

Closer . . . closer . . . closer! She reached out with her long neck, trying to catch the net between her

teeth. But just as she was about to catch it, the wind snatched it and sent it spiraling toward Dewdrop Spring.

"Oh no! It mustn't land in the water!" Daisy cried. "We'll never get the moonbeams back if it does."

She dived down, swooping toward the surface of the spring. The wind suddenly dropped, and the net began to fall down . . . down . . . down. . . .

"I'm going to be too late!"
Daisy puffed.

She flapped her wings as
hard as she could and zoomed
after it. She wouldn't give up! As
she opened her mouth to grab the
net with her teeth, she heard a
big *SPLASH*. She'd gotten it! But
what was that splash? Had the
moonbeams fallen out?

CHAPTER FIVE

A Special Visitor

Daisy rose up away from Dewdrop Spring and circled around to find Maddy and Herbie, who were just catching up.

"You did it!" Maddy cheered.

"Yes," said Daisy, passing her the net. "But I'm really sorry—I think I lost some of your moonbeams. I heard them splashing into the water."

"No, no," squealed Herbie. "We saw it all. It wasn't the moonbeams that splashed into the water—it was your hooves!"

Daisy felt her heart leap. She was so relieved!

"Thank you, thank you!" Maddy squeaked, fluttering around Daisy. "Now I'd better go and make up for lost time. Maybe I can still win the competition!"

"Yes, yes, go go go!" Daisy exclaimed. "And good luck!"

As Maddy raced off, Daisy looked down. Her legs and hoofs were dripping with water, so she shook them one by one to dry them, then turned to Herbie.

"You *must* be tired by now, Herbie," she said. "That was a lot of flying, wasn't it?"

Herbie's eyes were beginning to droop. He put one paw up to his mouth to hide a yawn. "Yes, it was. But I'm not tired." He blinked, then tried to open his eyes wide. "Not even a tiny bit."

"Are you sure?" Daisy asked gently. "Wouldn't you like to snuggle down to sleep?"

"No! I told you—I'm never
going to sleep again," Herbie
insisted, hiding another yawn.

Daisy gave her fur one last

85

shake, and smiled. "Oh yes, you did say that. Well, we'd better do something else, then. How about we go back to Heather Hill?"

Herbie looked at her suspiciously. "But that's where I usually go to sleep for the night," he said. "You're not going to make me go to bed, are you?"

"No, no, of course not," Daisy said soothingly. "I need to find some more fairy animals to deliver

86

dreams to, that's all. You can help

me do that."

Herbie nodded. "All right,

then."

Daisy sniffed the cool air and

fluttered her wings. It was her

favorite time of night. The stars

were twinkling merrily, and the

moon was at its brightest. It was

when she felt her most lively—but

she could see that poor Herbie was

struggling. As they took off once

more, his wings would only beat
very slowly—so slowly that he
could hardly stay in the air!

"It's not too far," Daisy said.

"We'll fly back up past Golden Meadow, and you can have a rest every now and then if you want."

"I . . . don't . . . need . . . to . . . rest," said Herbie, but even his voice sounded slow.

Daisy felt so sorry for him. She wished he would believe that there was no such thing as a Hedgehog Gobbler, but he was much too frightened. What could she do?

They flew up the valley, past tall, waving poplar trees, gnarled old oaks, and blossoming hedgerows. They were about halfway up when Daisy thought she heard a strange whooshing sound. She glanced at Herbie. Could it be his tired wings making a funny noise?

But then Herbie heard it, too. "What's that noise?" he demanded. "Is it the Hedgehog Gobbler?"

The whooshing was getting louder, and louder, and LOUDER!

"It is!" Herbie yelled. "It really is the Gobbler this time!"

Daisy didn't know what to say. The whooshing sound was definitely very strange and scary, and she didn't know *what* it could be. She gestured at Herbie to fly down to the ground.

"Here it comes!" shrieked Herbie, making Daisy jump.

They cowered as a huge creature flew toward them. It had massive dark wings and enormous eyes. Even Daisy was frightened this time—it definitely wasn't a tree or a net of flying moonbeams!

"Who are you?" she called out bravely.

The creature swooped past them and landed on the branch of a sycamore tree. "I am the Wise Wishing Owl," it hooted.

"And tell me, whooooooooo are

yoooooou?"

Daisy and Herbie heaved a sigh

of relief, then looked at each other in

amazement. The Wise Wishing Owl?

She was the oldest, wisest creature

in all of Misty Wood, and the fairy

animals rarely saw her!

"I thought you were the

Hedgehog Gobbler!" exclaimed

Herbie. "I'm so glad you're not."

The Wise Wishing Owl ruffled

94

her feathers. "The Hedgehog what?" she hooted.

"The Hedgehog Gobbler," said Herbie, fluttering up toward the beautiful owl. "It's really big, even bigger than you, and ten times scarier," he explained breathlessly. "It's got huge teeth and a ginormous belly, and it comes out at night to find hedgehogs who are curled up fast asleep. And then it gobbles them up whole!"

"Is that so?" the Wise Wishing Owl said, gazing at him with her big round eyes.

"Yes! Yes!" said Herbie. "We've been trying to escape from it all night!"

"Oh, dear." The Wise Wishing Owl looked at Herbie gravely. "Tell me something, young hedgehog. I have lived in Misty Wood longer than any other creature, but I have never, ever heard of or seen a

96

Hedgehog Gobbler. So how do you

explain that?"

"I don't know." Herbie frowned.

"But I do know that he's out there

and that I mustn't ever go to sleep again."

The Wise Wishing Owl gave a soft chuckle. "All right," she said. "Tell me something else. Who told you about the Hedgehog Gobbler?"

"My big brother, Horace," said Herbie.

The Wise Wishing Owl nodded. "I thought it might be someone like that. Now, does Horace ever play tricks on you?"

98

"Oh yes," said Herbie. "We play tricks on each other all the time. He loves hiding my breakfast or jumping out at me from behind a tree, so then I pretend to be a spiny dragon to scare him or . . ." Suddenly, his eyes opened wide. "Do you—do you think the story about the Hedgehog Gobbler is one of his tricks?"

The Wise Wishing Owl smiled and nodded. "Yes, from what I

know about big brothers, I think
it most certainly is. Now, what
do you think he'd say if he knew
you'd stayed up all night worrying
about it?"

Herbie's cheeks went pink. "Oh!
He'd really laugh." He looked at
Daisy, then the owl, then back to
Daisy. "He'd better not find out."

"That's right," agreed the Wise
Wishing Owl, winking at Daisy.
Daisy smiled and nodded.

"In that case, I'd better get back to Heather Hill as fast as possible," said Herbie. "I've got a lot of sleeping to do!"

"Thank you, Wise Wishing Owl," said Daisy. "I'm so glad we've sorted out the mystery of the Hedgehog Gobbler at last!"

She and Herbie waved good-bye to the beautiful owl and rose up into the starry sky. Herbie managed to find one last burst of energy, and he

sailed along on the breeze singing to himself.

"There's no Hedgehog Gobbler," he warbled. "There's *nooo* Hedgehog Gobbler!"

Daisy chased after him, chuckling to herself, until Heather Hill was in sight. They swooped down to the old oak tree—the very same tree that she had found Herbie beside at the beginning of the night.

Herbie landed among the roots

and snuggled down. He curled into a ball, then looked up at Daisy with his eyelids drooping. "Thank you, Daisy," he said drowsily. "You've been a really good friend to me tonight."

"Oh, that's all right," said

Daisy. "You've been a big help to me, too. Perhaps we could have another adventure together one day."

But Herbie didn't reply. He had tucked his nose between his paws, and he was already fast asleep!

CHAPTER SIX

The Best Dream Ever

Daisy smiled to herself. "Now it's
Herbie's turn for the best dream
ever," she murmured. "Let's see . . ."

Daisy thought of all the things

she had learned about Herbie. She leaned close to his tiny ear and began. "You're out in the woods with your friends," she whispered. "You're all having loads of fun doing your special job, collecting leaves with your prickles to make Misty Wood nice and tidy. While you're working, you play hide-and-seek, and you hide so cleverly that no one can find you for the longest time!"

Daisy gazed down at Herbie and saw a happy smile curling up the corners of his mouth.

"And then, tucked into your hiding place, you spot something really tasty," she went on. "It's a big pile of shiny brown hazelnuts. When your friends find you at last, you show them what you've found and you all decide to have a hazelnut party!"

Herbie gave a tiny squeak of

excitement and twitched his nose in his sleep.

"You share all your hazelnuts with your friends and, to say thank you, they sing you a song. And then you all begin to dance."

As Herbie wriggled happily in his sleep, Daisy fetched some leaves to cover him so that he was even cozier than before. Then she slipped away quietly into the night, leaving him to his lovely dream.

With the moon beginning to dip down in the sky, she knew she had no time to waste—she wanted

to go and see how Maddy was doing.

Daisy flew back down the valley toward Moonshine Pond. As she went, she realized that the wind had finally dropped, and the trees and hedgerows lay still and silent under the sparkling stars.

At least Maddy won't lose her net now, Daisy thought. *Maybe she'll have managed to catch her final moonbeams just in time.*

By the time she arrived at the
pond, all the moles had finished
work for the night. They were
gathering on the banks by
the willow trees, holding their
moonbeam nets. The competition
must be over already! Daisy rushed
forward to see what was happening.
Where was Maddy? And who had
won?

And then she spotted her
friend. She was standing right at

111

the top of the bank by a fallen
tree trunk. Meredith, the oldest
Moonbeam Mole of Misty Wood,
was standing on the trunk as if it
were a stage—and she was making
an announcement.

"And the winner of our special
brambleberry crumble competition
is . . . Maddy!" she exclaimed.
"Maddy, please step forward to
show everyone your net!"

Maddy looked as though she

would burst with pride. She hopped onto the tree trunk and waved her net, which was bulging with all her moonbeams.

"Well done, Maddy. You were the first mole to collect one hundred moonbeams," Meredith said, smiling at her. "And now here's your special prize."

Daisy and all the moles clapped and cheered. Maddy bowed to everyone before accepting

113

DAISY THE DEER

the delicious dessert. The smell of
the crumble wafted over to Daisy,
and her mouth began to water. She
was so happy for her friend.

"Now, I know that Maddy
will be dying to taste her prize,"
said Meredith. "But first, there's
an important job to do. We have
all worked very, very hard tonight
collecting our moonbeams. And
now it's time to place them where
they belong—in Moonshine Pond.

So, Maddy, as our winner, would you please lead the way?"

Maddy nodded eagerly. She put her crumble down on the tree-trunk stage to keep it safe, then fluttered up and above the water with her net. She tilted the net and tipped out the moonbeams. They rippled gently into the water, lighting it up with a soft pearly glow. All the other Moonbeam Moles did the same, until

Moonshine Pond glistened and shimmered more beautifully than Daisy had ever seen before in her life. It looked amazing!

"Well done, Maddy!" Daisy called out.

"Daisy!" Maddy exclaimed happily, trotting back up the bank. "Come on—you have to help me eat my crumble!"

"Oh, no," said Daisy. "You won it—it's all yours!"

"Don't be silly," Maddy said with a smile. "If you hadn't caught my net for me, I never would have won. And anyway, there's far too much of it for just me."

Daisy grinned. "Well, if you're sure," she said. "Thank you!"

Together, they fetched the crumble and sat down by the trees to eat it. As Daisy took her first bite, she closed her eyes. It was the yummiest crumble ever.

"Mmmmmm," she mumbled.

"Mmmm-mmmm!" agreed
Maddy.

Their mouths were too full to
say anything else!

Daisy gazed over to the east, where the first hint of dawn was turning the sky from purple-black to deep blue. What a night of adventure it had been! As the crumble settled down into her tummy, she began to feel all warm and sleepy. She thought of Herbie enjoying his lovely dream, and smiled as she remembered how hard he'd tried to stay awake. Soon it would be bedtime for her, too,

but she was quite sure that she wouldn't have Herbie's problem. Oh no! She was so tired and happy, it would only be seconds before she was fast . . . asleep. . . .

121

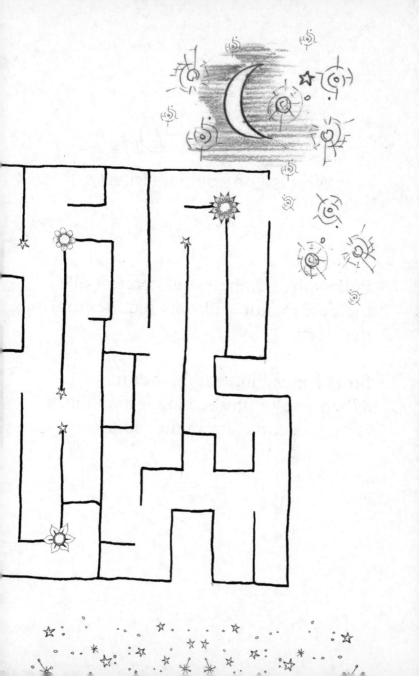

Connect the Dots

Who is the special visitor?

Follow the numbers and connect all the dots to make a lovely picture from the story.

Start connecting with dot number 1. When you've finished joining all the dots, you can color in the picture!

Draw a Special Dream for Daisy

Daisy's special job is to give dreams to the sleeping fairy animals of Misty Wood.

But can you give Daisy a special dream while she is sleeping?

Fairy Animals

of Misty Wood

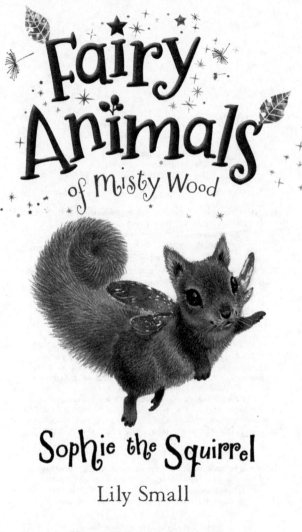

Sophie the Squirrel

Lily Small

Henry Holt and Company
New York

With special thanks to Gill Harvey

Henry Holt and Company
Publishers since 1866
175 Fifth Avenue
New York, NY 10010
mackids.com

First published in the United States in 2017 by Henry Holt and Company.
Originally published in Great Britain in 2014 by Egmont UK Limited.

Library of Congress Cataloging-in-Publication Data

Names: Small, Lily, author.
Title: Sophie the Squirrel : Fairy Animals of Misty Wood / Lily Small.
New York : Henry Holt and Company,
2017. | Series: Fairy animals of Misty Wood | Summary: Sophie the
Stardust Squirrel is sure it is her fault when she and her friends
practice a special dance for the Misty Wood fair and things go wrong.
Identifiers: LCCN 2016048093 (print) | LCCN 2017017223 (ebook) |
ISBN 978-1-250-29718-1 (Paper Over Board)
Subjects: | CYAC: Fairies—Fiction. | Magic—Fiction. | Squirrels—Fiction. |
Self-confidence—Fiction. | Dance—Fiction. | BISAC: JUVENILE FICTION /
Fantasy & Magic. | JUVENILE FICTION / Social Issues / Friendship.
Classification: LCC PZ7.S6385 (ebook) | LCC PZ7.S6385 Sop 2017 (print) |
DDC [E]—dc23
LC record available at https://lccn.loc.gov/2016048093

Our books may be purchased in bulk for promotional, educational, or business use.
Please contact your local bookseller or the Macmillan Corporate
and Premium Sales Department at (800) 221-7945 ext. 5442
or by e-mail at MacmillanSpecialMarkets@macmillan.com.

First American Edition—2017
Printed in the United States of America by
LSC Communications, Harrisonburg, Virginia

1 3 5 7 9 10 8 6 4 2

Contents

Chapter One
Rise and Shine!   1

Chapter Two
Practice Makes Perfect   16

Chapter Three
Hello, Mr. Bluebird!   41

Chapter Four
Triple Trouble   58

Chapter Five
Shooting Star!   73

Chapter Six
The Big Day   89

Chapter Seven
Rainbow Bright!   107

CHAPTER ONE

Rise and Shine!

Misty Wood was brimming over
with excitement. The sun was
beaming happily as he stretched
his rays out to every corner of the

wood. The leaves on the trees were rustling cheerfully. The blooms in the meadows were bobbing their heads joyfully in the breeze. And everywhere you looked, fairy animals were fluttering their sparkling wings and whispering behind their paws.

"Tomorrow is the fair!" they chattered. "Tomorrow is the *fair*!"

High up in an old oak tree, a pretty little face popped out of

a hole in the trunk. The face was followed by a silky red body with sparkly violet wings. Last of all came a bushy golden tail that twitched to and fro. It was Sophie the Stardust Squirrel.

"Tomorrow is going to be the best day of my whole life!" she cried. "I can't wait, I can't wait!" Sophie was especially excited because she and her friends had been chosen to perform the opening

4

dance at the Misty Wood fair
this year.

Sophie hopped onto a branch
and smoothed down her whiskers.
Then she flexed her fairy wings
and closed her eyes, imagining
what tomorrow would be like.

The opening dance of the Misty
Wood fair was always lovely. Every
year, some clever Bark Badgers
made a wooden festival pole, carved
with woodland scenes and beautiful

swirling patterns. It was placed in the middle of a big, grassy clearing, then brightly colored strands of flowers were attached like ribbons to stream down from the top. Each dancer held a strand and skipped around the pole.

Today the pole would finally be ready, and Sophie and her friends would get the chance to have one last practice.

Sophie jiggled her tail at the

very thought and scampered down
the old oak tree. She was so excited,
she couldn't stay still! When she
reached the bottom, she jumped back
up again, imagining that the tree
was the pole. As she twisted
and turned around the gnarled
trunk, she thought of all the other
fairy animals, cheering loudly as she
and her friends performed the dance.

Just as she reached the top of the
tree, she heard someone shouting.

"What's all that scraping and scuffling?" Sophie's mom called.

Sophie peered down through the branches. Her mom was poking her head out of the nest in the cozy hollow where they lived, looking this way and that.

"It's only me, Mom," Sophie replied.

"Sophie! Whatever are you up to?" asked her mom, looking up at her. "You're making so much noise that you woke poor Sammy from his nap."

"Oh, I'm sorry, Mom!" Sophie exclaimed. Sammy was Sophie's little brother. He was still very young, so he always had a midday snooze. "I didn't mean to wake him. I'm just so excited about tomorrow."

Sophie's mom smiled. "Yes, I understand. I remember dancing at the fair when I was your age. It was so much fun. But try not to get *too* excited, Sophie—look at what you've done to our tree!"

10

"Done? I haven't done anything . . ." Sophie began. But as she looked around the branches, she clapped her paw to her mouth. The old oak tree was shimmering silver from head to foot! The leaves were no longer green. The trunk was no longer brown. Every single part of the tree was covered in stardust!

Like all the other fairy animals in Misty Wood, Stardust Squirrels

11

had their own special job. Their big, bushy tails sprinkled stardust whenever the squirrels gave them a shake. They were supposed to scatter the dust lightly over Misty Wood so that it twinkled gently. But the oak tree wasn't just twinkling now. It was *glowing*!

"Never mind," chuckled Sophie's mom. "The next time it rains it will all get washed away. And, in the meantime, it's quite

nice having the brightest tree in the whole wood—at least we'll be able to find our way home in the dark! Now it's time you went to your practice."

"Oh! Is it?" Sophie sat up on her back legs and wiggled her whiskers.

Sophie's mom nodded.

"Hurray!" cheered Sophie. "We're going to dance around the festival pole at last!" With

13

two enormous flicks of her tail, she bounded down the tree, scattering more stardust. She looked up at her mom to wave good-bye. "Uh-oh . . ." she murmured.

Her mom's head had turned silver now, too. It was hard to tell where she ended and the tree began!

Sophie's mom laughed and gave her head a shake, sending a cloud of stardust shimmering to the ground.

14

"Good luck," she called. "And be careful what you do with that tail!"

"I will," Sophie said with a grin. "See you later, Mom." And with a flutter of her fairy wings, she flew off to find her friends.

15

CHAPTER TWO

Practice Makes Perfect

Sophie rose up above the trees,

enjoying the feel of the breeze

ruffling her soft fur.

First of all she had to fetch

her friend Katie from Hawthorn Hedgerows.

It was a beautiful sunny day, and the delicious scent of hawthorn blossoms wafted toward Sophie as she swooped over the hedges. Soon

the glint of a shiny dewdrop caught
her eye, and she dived down to land
near a silvery cobweb.

"Katie!" she called. "Where are
you?"

"I'm over here!" a tinkly voice
meowed.

Sophie peeked over the cobweb
and spotted her friend's tabby fur
and silvery wings. Katie was a
Cobweb Kitten. It was the Cobweb
Kittens' job to collect dewdrops

18

every morning from Dewdrop

Spring, then use them to decorate

the cobwebs in Misty Wood.

Sophie watched as Katie fished

a dewdrop from her little basket and

balanced it perfectly on one of the cobweb's delicate threads.

"Almost finished!" said Katie. "Only two more to go!"

"Good," said Sophie. "It's time for our final dance practice."

"I know," Katie purred. "I was so excited this morning, I kept dropping my dewdrops! That's why I haven't quite finished yet."

"I can help you," Sophie offered. "Shall we place one each?"

Katie gave a big smile. "Yes, please!" She pointed a snowy white paw to the top of a nearby hedge. "Could you put one on that tiny cobweb over there?"

Sophie nodded eagerly. Then she bounded forward and scooped a dewdrop from Katie's basket. It glimmered like a precious diamond in her paws. Holding it carefully, she carried it over to the cobweb. She felt honored to be helping

Katie do her job. Sophie placed the dewdrop on the silky strand of web and hopped back.

"Ooh, thank you, Sophie—that looks lovely," Katie said.

Sophie turned to Katie and smiled. "Come on, then, let's go and get Bonnie."

The two friends fluttered off toward Honeydew Meadow. Bonnie was a Bud Bunny. The Bud Bunnies' special job was to nudge

22

the flower buds into bloom by twitching their noses against them. Now, thanks to their hard work, the meadow was bursting with all the colors of the rainbow.

Sophie and Katie hovered over the sea of color for a moment, looking for their friend. Then, in the middle of a patch of pale blue flowers, Sophie spotted Bonnie's sparkly pink wings and soft white fur.

"There she is!" Sophie cried. "She's just about to open another flower."

Bonnie was sitting perfectly

24

still with her nose very close to
a nodding flower bud. As Sophie
and Katie watched, Bonnie's
nose twitched . . . and one by one,
the petals of the flower burst open.

Sophie and Katie flew down
to land beside Bonnie, clapping
their paws. Bonnie's long white ears
pricked up at the sight of her two
friends.

"Hi, Bonnie! Your flowers
are so pretty," Sophie said. "Are

you ready to come to our dance practice?"

Bonnie twirled her whiskers. "Ooh, is it time?" she asked.

Sophie and Katie nodded.

"I'd better just tell my mom. She's working over there," said Bonnie, waving her paw in the direction of some brightly colored tulips.

Bonnie's mom was sitting in the middle of the tulips, twitching

26

her nose against one of the glossy buds. The friends scampered up to her just as the tulip burst into bloom. Its petals were as yellow and shiny as the sun.

"Mom, can I go to my dance practice?" Bonnie asked.

"Of course." Bonnie's mom smiled at the little fairy animals, and her fluffy cotton tail began thumping on the ground. "I have a nice surprise for you, too."

27

"Ooh, I love surprises!" Sophie exclaimed, and her tail twitched, sending a puff of stardust into the air.

"What kind of surprise is it?" Bonnie asked, hopping around to catch some stardust on the tips of her ears.

Bonnie's mom smoothed back her whiskers and leaned toward them. "I'm going to make each of you a flower garland to wear when

you do your dance at the fair," she said. "I'm going to use the prettiest flowers in all of Misty Wood's meadows!"

Sophie was so pleased, her wings started fluttering. As she rose into the air, her tail twitched this way and that, showering stardust all over the tulips.

"Thank you!" she cried.

"Thank you!" Bonnie and Katie chorused.

"You're welcome," Bonnie's mom said with a smile.

"Now we just have to go and get Polly," Sophie said.

"Have fun!" Bonnie's mom called as she hopped over to a big cluster of crimson poppy buds and began nudging them open.

Sophie, Katie, and Bonnie swooped away, heading toward Dandelion Dell. It wasn't very far, and soon they could see golden

dandelions spread out like a carpet of sunshine below them.

The Pollen Puppies were hard at work, bouncing from one patch of blooms to another, wagging their tails as they went. They were doing a very important job—with each wag of their tails, they spread pollen so that there would be even more dandelions next year.

The three friends fluttered around in circles, looking for Polly.

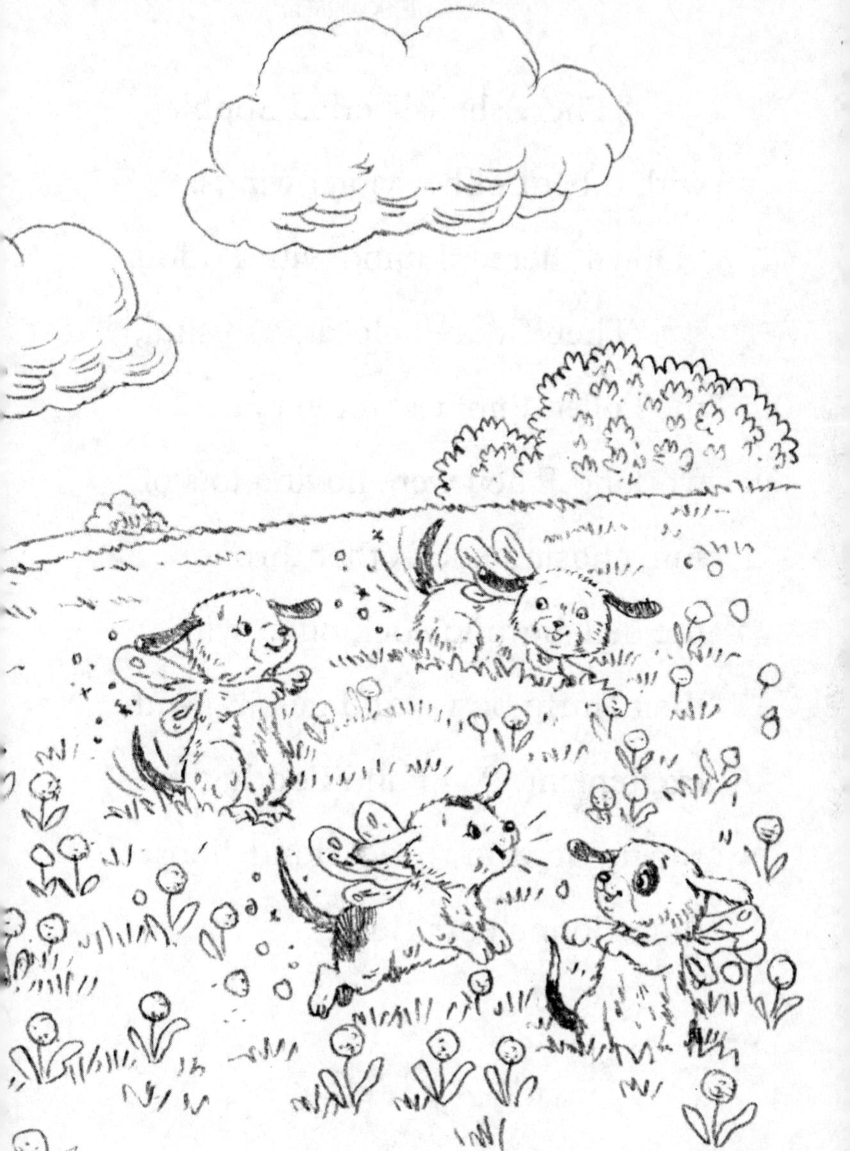

"There she is!" cried Sophie with a beat of her violet wings. "Down there, playing with Paddy."

They floated closer. As usual, the Pollen Puppies weren't *just* working. They were having lots of fun, chasing each other through the dell, batting each other with their fluffy paws, and yelping with excitement. Polly and Paddy were racing down a row of dandelions, their floppy ears flying.

"Polly!" called Katie, fluttering down to land. "It's time for our last dance practice."

Polly skidded to a halt next to a tall, tufty dandelion. "Oh!" she cried. "Is it really?" She clapped her paws, and her coppery brown tail wagged harder than ever.

Sophie, Katie, and Bonnie gathered around.

"Sorry, Paddy," said Polly. "I have to go now. Do you think

you can finish the rest on your own?"

"Of course!" Paddy panted, his little pink tongue hanging out. "But first I'm going to race my tail."

"How do you race your own tail?" Sophie asked with a frown.

"Easy peasy," Paddy replied. "Look!" And with that, he bounded off, his tail wagging so fast it became a golden blur.

Polly smoothed down her ears and rustled her golden wings. "I'm ready," she told the others. "Let's go!"

Sophie, Katie, Bonnie, and Polly flew off across the dell and

into the Heart of Misty Wood.

As they soared through the trees,
Sophie's wings flapped faster and
faster—she couldn't wait to see the
festival pole. But when they got to
the clearing where the dance was
supposed to take place, there was
no pole to be seen.

They fluttered down to the
ground and looked around. An old
Bark Badger with silvery wings was
busy carving beautiful patterns

into the bark of a nearby tree. They scampered over to him.

"Excuse me," Sophie said. "Do you know where the festival pole is? We've been chosen to perform the opening dance at the fair tomorrow, and we need to practice."

The badger stopped what he was doing and smiled at Sophie. "I'm sorry, little Stardust Squirrel, but the pole isn't quite ready yet," he said. "My badger friends are

39

sick, so I am decorating it all on my own. It won't be ready until tomorrow morning."

"But the fair starts in the morning!" Sophie gasped.

The four friends looked at one another. They had worked out all their steps. They'd gone through them so many times that they knew them by heart. But they'd never practiced with ribbons and a pole. What were they going to do?

CHAPTER THREE

Hello, Mr. Bluebird!

Sophie rubbed her nose with her paw. "We'll have to find a different kind of pole," she said, "and pretend that it's the proper one."

"Yes," Katie agreed. "There has to be something that will do, somewhere in Misty Wood."

They sat in a huddle and tried to think. What would be tall and strong and ribbony enough to make a good practice pole? They scratched their heads and tugged their whiskers. But it was no use— they couldn't think of anything.

"Maybe we should just go and look for one," Sophie said at last.

"Yes," said Bonnie. "But we'll have to be quick. We'll never be ready by tomorrow if we don't find one soon!"

They unfurled their wings and flew off together to begin the hunt. They soared over Hawthorn Hedgerows, but there were only twigs and bushes there. Then they made for Honeydew Meadow, but they could see only pretty flowers.

Next, they glided around the

Heart of Misty Wood, but the trees there were too tall and tangly. When they flew over Moonshine Pond, they saw lots of dragonflies, but they didn't see anything that looked like a good practice pole.

"What are we going to *do*?" wailed Katie, her tabby tail drooping.

"Let's try Dewdrop Spring," Sophie said.

"But that's just water," said

44

Katie sadly. "I've never seen anything like a pole there."

Sophie knew that her friend was probably right. But they couldn't give up—not until they had searched all of Misty Wood. As they fluttered toward Dewdrop Spring, Sophie spotted something in the distance that made her heart leap.

"Look!" she exclaimed, pointing down. "It's perfect!"

There, on the bank of the

45

spring, stood an elegant willow tree. Its trunk was tall and straight, but its thin branches swept down all around it—just like ribbons.

"Oh yes, of course," purred Katie happily. "Well done, Sophie!"

"Hurray!" cried Bonnie.

Polly yapped gleefully and did a loop-the-loop, then zoomed down to the willow tree at full speed. Giggling and chattering, the other three followed her. They skipped

HELLO, MR. BLUEBIRD!

around the tree, deciding which branches would make the best ribbons.

Suddenly, they heard a voice.

"What's all that noise around my tree?" it twittered.

The four friends fell silent at once. They squinted up into the willow tree.

"It's only . . . only . . . us . . ." Sophie began, peering through the branches. She couldn't see anything

at first, but then, right at the top
of the tree, she spied a little nest.
And perched on the nest was a
bluebird, with feathers the color of
a bright summer sky.

"We're sorry, Mr. Bluebird," Sophie said. "It's the Misty Wood fair tomorrow, and we're performing the opening dance—but we don't have a pole to practice with. Your tree is the only thing we've found. Would you mind if we use it, just for a little while?"

The bluebird hopped out of his nest and flew down to the ground.

"The opening dance, eh?" he chirped, tilting his head.

50

"Yes," Sophie said, nodding.

"That sounds very important," tweeted the bluebird. "Important enough for you to use my tree. But won't you need some music to dance to?"

"Oh yes," said Bonnie. "We'll have music tomorrow. The Moss Mouse band will be playing for us while we dance."

"But what about now?" asked the bluebird. "How are you going

51

to practice if you don't have any music *now*?"

Sophie, Katie, Bonnie, and Polly looked at each other. The bluebird was right. They couldn't *really* know how the dance would go if they'd never tried it with music.

"Well . . ." said Sophie slowly, twitching her whiskers. She was beginning to feel a bit nervous. "I suppose we'll just have to hope for the best."

"No, no, no," chirped the bluebird, shaking his head. "That won't do at all. You *must* practice with music. And I know exactly what music you should have."

"You do?" Polly looked at him hopefully and her tail began to wag.

"It just so happens that I'm one of the best singers in the whole of Misty Wood," said the bluebird proudly. "So, as you've come to *my* tree and want to dance under *my*

53

nest, I think I should help the four of you out."

"Really?" Sophie gasped. "You'll sing for us?"

The bluebird puffed out his feathery chest. "I certainly will. Are you ready?"

Fumbling in excitement, the friends scampered around the tree, quickly deciding on which willow branches to use. When each of them was holding a branch, the bluebird

spread his wings, threw back his head, and began to sing in a sweet, soaring voice.

It was the most beautiful song that any of them had ever heard. They danced in time, weaving in and out of one another around the tree. First one way, then another, and then . . .

"Ow!" cried Sophie, stopping with a bump.

The bluebird stopped singing

and flew over to her. "What is it, little squirrel?" he asked.

"It's my tail," gasped Sophie. "I can't move it!"

Sophie's friends gathered around.

"It's all tangled up in the branches," Katie meowed.

Sophie pulled her tail one way. Then she pulled it the other way. But it was no use. She was well and truly stuck!

56

CHAPTER FOUR
Triple Trouble

"Oh no!" Sophie cried. "How can we practice for the dance if I'm stuck to the tree?" She looked at her friends, her brown eyes widened

in fear. "What if I'm stuck here forever?"

"Don't worry." Bonnie hopped over and patted Sophie with her paw. "We'll soon figure it out."

"We just need to be patient," Katie agreed. "We'll untangle it one branch at a time."

"I'll sing you a patient song, if you like," the little bluebird chirped, perching himself on a branch in

front of Sophie. He began tweeting very slowly and gently.

Polly, Bonny, and Katie began working on Sophie's tail. Slowly and gently, in time with the song, they untwisted the long, thin willow branches one by one. Sophie watched them anxiously over her shoulder. Sometimes they accidentally pulled her fur, and she had to try hard not to yelp. To take her mind off it, she closed her

eyes and thought of yummy acorns instead.

Just as Sophie was thinking of her twenty-second acorn, Polly clapped her paws.

"You're free!" she woofed.

Sophie opened her eyes. The

bluebird was flying around and around in a circle, chirping wildly.

Sophie hopped forward. It felt so good to be able to move again. "Thank you!" she exclaimed in relief. "And don't worry, I'll be doubly careful with my tail from now on!"

They all took their positions around the tree, and the bluebird flew up to the top.

"All ready?" he called down.

62

"Yes!" they chorused.

He opened his little beak and began his beautiful song again. The dance started, and soon Sophie had forgotten all about trapping her tail. As she and her friends skipped in time with the bluebird's melody she felt herself getting more and more excited.

Tomorrow is going to be so wonderful, Sophie thought to herself. *It's going to be the best day of my—*

"*AAAHHH . . . CHOO!*"

Sophie jumped as a loud sneeze rang out across the banks of the spring. Then it got even worse.

"*AAAHHH . . . CHOO! Cough, cough, COUGH!*"

Sophie stopped dancing and looked around. Bonnie was doubled over behind her. Her floppy ears were lying flat and her pink eyes were streaming.

"Oh no!" gulped Sophie.

She could see at once what the problem was. Bonnie's normally snowy white fur was glimmering silver. Sophie had gotten so excited while she'd been dancing that she'd showered Bonnie in stardust!

"*Cough cough cough*," spluttered Bonnie. "I've got stardust up my— *aaahhh . . . choo*—nose."

"I'm so sorry," cried Sophie. "Oh dear, my tail's causing all sorts of problems today."

Polly let go of her branch and bounded over. "Don't worry," she yapped. "I'll soon fix it."

She scampered around Bonnie, wagging her tail, just as she did when she was flicking pollen in the meadows. *Flick flick flick*, went her tail. *Flick flick flickety flick . . .*

Bonnie started to giggle. "It tickles!" she cried as Polly's tail flicked away at her fur.

The bluebird flew above them,

TRIPLE TROUBLE

chirping jauntily, and soon Polly
had flicked all the stardust away.

"Oh, well done, Polly!" Sophie
exclaimed. "You've done a really
great job!"

"Yes, thanks, Polly," agreed
Bonnie, wiping her eyes dry. "I'm
ready to start dancing again."

"Right," said Sophie. "And
this time my tail won't cause any
problems. I won't let it!"

So off around the tree they

went. Sophie concentrated really hard. She mustn't shake her tail too much, and she mustn't get it stuck.

"I'll tuck it between my legs," she muttered to herself.

As the practice went on, Sophie began to feel happier and more confident. With her tail tucked tightly between her legs, there were no more problems. But just as they whirled around the tree

one last time, Sophie suddenly felt herself hurtling forward.

"Wahhhhhh!" she cried.

THUMP. She fell flat on her face.

"Help!" squeaked Bonnie, bumping into Sophie.

"Uh-oh!" yelped Polly, landing on Bonnie's back.

"Oh no!" meowed Katie, falling head over heels on top of them all!

"Oh no, oh no, oh no!" the

bluebird tweeted as he hovered
above.

The four fairy animals lay in
a heap on the ground, their paws,

wings, and tails in a higgledy-piggledy jumble. Sophie lay at the bottom of the pile, trying to work out what had happened. And then she realized. She'd tucked her tail so tightly between her legs that she'd tripped right over it!

A big, fat tear rolled down Sophie's cheek. "It's all my fault," she wept. "Everything's going wrong, and I'll never be able to get the dance right. *Never!*"

72

CHAPTER FIVE

Shooting Star!

A delicious smell wafted through
the cozy hollow in the old oak tree.
It was Sophie's favorite dinner—
acorn soup—and her dad had just

finished making it. But Sophie didn't feel hungry at all. Her baby brother banged his wooden spoon and gurgled impatiently, but Sophie was quite sure that she wouldn't be able to eat even the tiniest bit. She sat on her little sycamore stool in the corner, feeling glum.

"What's the matter?" Sophie's mom asked. "Didn't your practice go well?"

Sophie shook her head. "No,

it didn't." She could feel her lip beginning to wobble.

"Oh, never mind," her dad said with a smile. "It can't have been that bad."

"But it *was*," Sophie cried. "Everyone's going to laugh at me at the fair. I can't dance at all!"

"Yes you can," said her dad. "You're a lovely dancer."

"Not anymore," Sophie said, her head drooping low.

75

Sophie's mom hopped over and stroked her silky fur. "What happened?"

"My tail spoiled everything," Sophie muttered. "First I got it stuck. Then it showered stardust all over Bonnie and made her cough and sneeze. And then I tripped over it—and everyone else tripped over me! Stupid tail!"

"Oh, dear," said Sophie's mom. She wrapped her own bushy tail

around Sophie in a big hug. "But try not to get too upset. Things always go wrong in rehearsals—I'm sure it will be fine at the fair."

Normally, her mom's hugs made Sophie feel a lot better. But not today. All she could think about was how terrible the dance was going to be. She started to cry, and buried her face in her paws.

"It's going . . . to be . . . awful," she sobbed.

"Now, don't you worry," her dad said, giving her one of his twinkly-eyed smiles. "I think I have an idea."

"You do?" Sophie peeked hopefully at him through her paws.

Sophie's dad whispered in her mom's ear, and her mom nodded, her eyes sparkling.

"Oh yes," her mom said in a mysterious voice. "That will work. Definitely!"

Sophie's dad winked at Sophie and beckoned to her. "Come on," he said. "You and I are going out."

"What . . . *now*?" It was dark

79

outside, and Sophie hardly ever went out at night.

Her dad nodded and held out his paw. "Follow me," he said.

Sophie felt a tiny bit nervous at first, going out in the dark, but she knew she was safe with her dad. He opened his strong red wings and led her up, up, up toward the glowing, pearly face of the moon.

Soon they were high above the

treetops, with nothing but twinkling stars around them. Sophie looked down and gasped. Misty Wood lay out like a map below her—it looked very beautiful in the moonlight. There were the flower buds in the meadows, drooping their little heads as they slept. There were the shimmering waters of Dewdrop Spring. Then Sophie saw flashes of pale light and pointed down excitedly.

"Look, Dad!" she cried.

The Moonbeam Moles were flitting through the darkness below them like shadows, catching glowing moonbeams to drop into Moonshine Pond. Sophie's dad nodded, then carried on flying upward. Sophie had to flap her wings very hard to be able to keep up with him.

"Why are we going so high?" she panted.

Her dad looked back at her and smiled. "It's just a little bit farther."

Sophie fluttered up next to him, panting from all the effort.

"This is what we've come for," her dad explained. "Look. Up there."

Sophie looked. Above her head, the most beautiful shooting star flew past, leaving a rainbow-colored trail of stardust behind it.

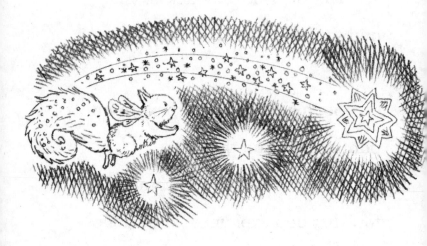

"Wow!" Sophie breathed.

"Now, be quick," her dad said.
"Fly after it and catch some of that
stardust in your tail."

84

Sophie twitched her bushy tail excitedly. All of a sudden she didn't feel tired at all. The star was the most lovely thing she'd ever seen! She whooshed after it.

The star danced across the sky, making wonderful patterns as it went. Sometimes it zigzagged or soared in spiraling circles. Sometimes it even made the shape of flower petals as it looped around the shining moon.

85

As Sophie chased the star, she twisted her tail this way and that to catch as much stardust as she could. She completely forgot all her worries about the dance practice. She even forgot about the fair. All she could think about was how happy she was to be out catching rainbow-colored stardust in her fluffy tail.

The shooting star did one last enormous loop, then it disappeared

behind the moon. Sophie gazed after it. Had it really gone? She felt a bit sad. Her dad flew up and placed his paw on her shoulder.

"Shooting stars never last long," he said, "and you did very well to catch so much stardust. You see, shooting-star dust is special."

"Really?" Sophie's eyes shone.

"Yes." Her dad smiled. "It is magical, and now that dust from a shooting star is in your tail, you'll

be able to get it to behave perfectly in the dance tomorrow."

Sophie twitched her ears in disbelief. "Really?"

"Really and truly." Her dad nodded solemnly. "As long as you believe in the magic . . ."

CHAPTER SIX

The Big Day

Dawn was breaking over Misty
Wood, spreading pale golden light
across the hedgerows and hills,
meadows and valleys.

Sophie opened her eyes. She gazed up at the cluster of oak leaves that dangled over her mossy bed, and frowned. A strange memory was taking shape in her head—or had it been a dream? Something about chasing a shooting star . . .

Sophie hopped out of bed and gave her tail a little shake. A puff of rainbow-colored stardust filled the air and drifted down onto her

soft pillow. Sophie gasped. It hadn't

been a dream at all!

Sophie scampered across the cozy hollow to join her mom, her dad, and Sammy at their breakfast table made from polished conkers.

"Good morning, Sophie," said her mom. "Come and have some porridge. You're going to need plenty of energy today!"

Sophie sat down and took a mouthful of porridge. She knew she had to eat, but she was starting to feel nervous. Was her dad right

about the shooting-star dust? Would her tail really be okay?

Sophie had eaten half her porridge when she heard excited chatter coming from outside.

"Sophie, are you ready?" she heard Polly yap.

"It's time to go," Katie meowed.

"It's almost time for the fair!" Bonnie called.

Sophie leaped up from the table, her tail twitching. A cloud of

the special stardust shimmered into the bowls of porridge, like rainbow-colored sugar.

"Whoops!" Sophie exclaimed.

"Yay!" Sammy cried, looking at the porridge with glee.

"Good luck," Sophie's dad said as Bonnie's, Katie's, and Polly's noses peeped into the hollow. "We'll see you there. And don't forget what I told you!" he added with a wink at Sophie.

"I won't," promised Sophie.

She took a deep breath and headed out to join her friends.

Buzzing with energy, the four friends spread their wings and flew out between the trees. It was still early, but lots of fairy animals were already busy, bustling about making preparations for the fair.

Sophie spotted Old Frannie the Fern Fox's tent, draped in garlands of copper beech leaves, where she

would sit telling fairy fortunes
all day. Just beyond that, Sophie
saw the Misty Wood bees hard at
work, building their fairground
honeycomb maze. Sophie loved
wandering around in the maze,
giggling with her friends as they got
lost in its endless twists and turns.

As they got closer to the Heart
of Misty Wood, Katie pointed at
the shimmering, swaying cobweb
tent, made from the silky threads

96

of hundreds of Misty Wood spiders. Inside the tent would be all sorts of stalls displaying the fairy animals' favorite treats.

Every year there was a *Guess How Many Blackberries* competition. There would be a cake stall laden with mounds of hazelnut cakes and honey buns, acorn pies and conker crunchies. Flowers from the meadows would brighten every corner and, once the Cobweb

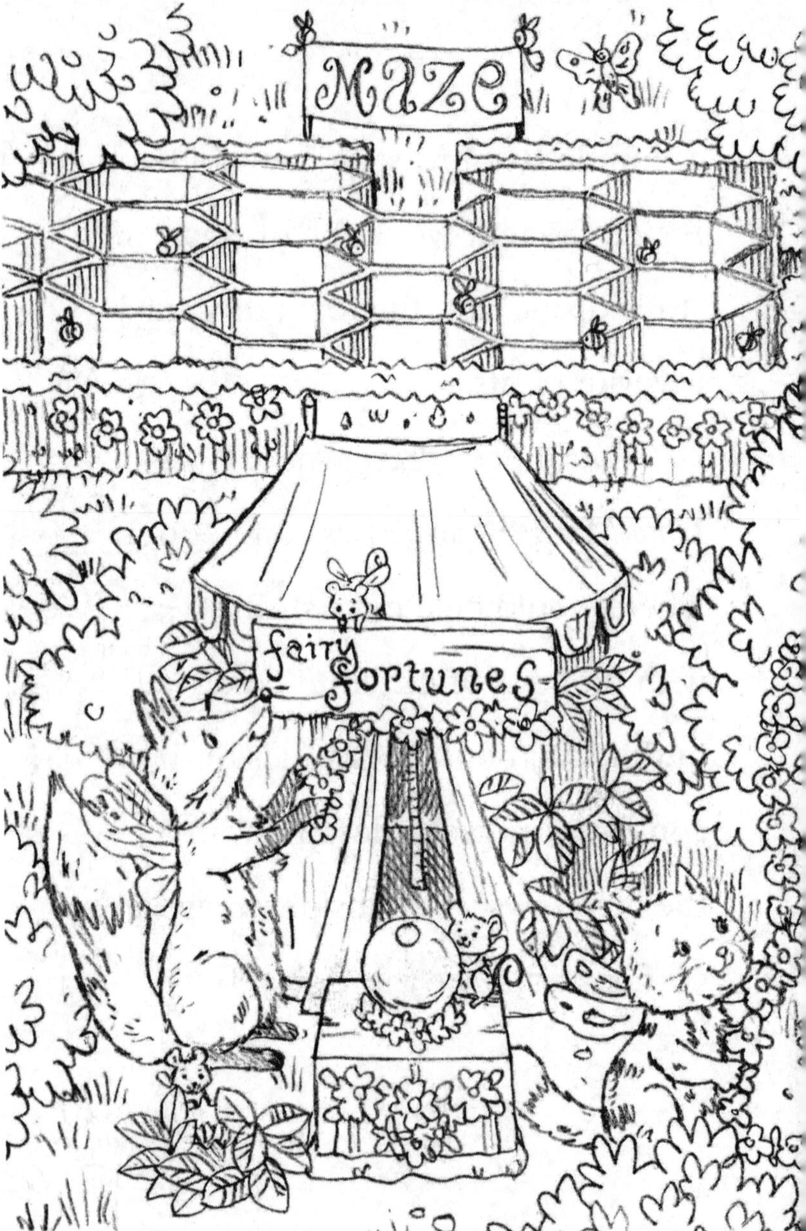
Maze
fairy fortunes

Kittens had gotten to work, the whole tent would be glistening with dewdrops from Dewdrop Spring!

Sophie couldn't wait for the fair to begin. It was all going to be so much fun!

They flew on toward the clearing where the grand opening was to take place. Sophie remembered that before they could explore any of the treats that the fair had in store, they had to

perform their dance. She started feeling a little nervous again. . . .

Down below, in the clearing, Sophie could see some Bark Badgers. They were gathered in a huddle, their silvery wings folded neatly over their striped black-and-white backs. They seemed to be having some kind of urgent meeting. Sophie suddenly felt worried. She couldn't see the festival pole anywhere. Where was

101

it? Shouldn't the badgers have put it in place by now?

Sophie and her friends fluttered down and scampered over to the badgers. "We're here!" Sophie cried. "We're ready to do our dance."

The badgers turned to them, their faces sad. Sophie's heart thudded. Now she knew for sure that something was wrong.

"Where's the festival pole?" she asked.

The badgers parted so that the four friends could see what they had been gathered around. There, on the vivid green grass, lay the festival pole covered in amazing carvings, with ribbons of flowers streaming from one end. Sophie's eyes shone when she saw how beautiful it was.

But then she noticed something. There was a problem. A *big* problem. The pole was broken in two, right in the middle.

"We just finished decorating it, but it was so heavy we dropped it," explained the badger they had met yesterday. He gave a long, sad sigh. "We're very, very sorry."

Sophie couldn't believe it. She blinked hard, hoping she might see something different when she opened her eyes—but the festival pole was still broken.

"So . . . what should we do now?" she asked in a very small voice.

"Well . . ." The badger stroked his chin and shuffled from one paw to the other. He looked very upset. "I'm afraid that there's nothing we can do. I'm very sorry, but the dance will just have to be canceled."

CHAPTER SEVEN

Rainbow Bright!

Canceled! Sophie rubbed her ears with her paws, hoping she had misheard.

The sun was peeping through

the trees around the clearing, and crowds of fairy animals had started to arrive. Over to one side, the Moss Mouse band had begun to play. There was no time left.

A tear rolled down Sophie's cheek. She sat down next to Polly, Bonnie, and Katie. They were all too sad to say anything. The other fairy animals who had begun to gather to watch the dance looked at them curiously.

Sophie thought about how wonderful everything had seemed last night, flying high in the dark sky, chasing the shooting star. She thought of practicing around the willow tree and how her dad had promised that the magical rainbow stardust would make her tail behave. None of that mattered anymore.

But as Sophie remembered all that had happened the day before,

an idea began to form in her mind.
She scrubbed her tears away and
leaped to her feet.

"I know what we're going to do!"
she called. "Everyone follow me!"

Polly's, Bonnie's, and Katie's

eyes widened, and they jumped
up excitedly.

"Where are we going?" asked
Katie.

"You'll soon find out," said
Sophie. "Come on, everyone!" she

called again to all the other fairy animals.

Sophie set off, half scampering, half fluttering, checking over her shoulder that everyone was following. Around the honeycomb maze, past the cobweb tent—she hurried on until she reached the banks of Dewdrop Spring.

The willow tree stood there, its branches draping down to the ground. Sophie bounded up to it.

She gave a shake of her tail, and
a little cloud of rainbow-colored
stardust puffed out. Then she flew
up and around the tree, shaking her
tail until the whole willow glittered
with glorious colors. Soon its trunk
glowed red, orange, and yellow,
and its branches looked like green,
purple, pink, and blue ribbons—
only even prettier!

"Wow!" gasped Katie, Bonnie,
and Polly as Sophie flew back.

113

"How did you do that?" Polly woofed, her tail wagging wildly. "It looks *beautiful*!"

"It's magic," Sophie said with a grin.

The fairy animals that had followed them began to flutter about, chattering to one another and spreading the news: The dance was back on! The Bark Badgers looked very relieved indeed.

As the crowd began to grow,

the band arrived and took their
places next to the tree. Just then,
Bonnie's mom appeared. Her paws
were full with the flower garlands
that she'd promised.

"Here you are!" she cried.
"You can't dance without your
garlands!"

She slipped one over Bonnie's
head. It was made of golden
buttercups and soft bluebells,
fluffy meadowsweet and bright red

poppies. It looked beautiful next to
the rainbow colors of the willow
tree. The crowd cheered and
clapped as Sophie, Katie, and Polly
put their garlands on, too.

Sophie's mom arrived and
flew over to give her a big, soft hug

with her bushy tail. The she joined
Sophie's dad and Sammy, right
at the front. They were all waving
excitedly. Sophie thought she might
burst with pride!

When all the animals had
gathered on the banks of the spring,
the band played a fanfare with
their lily trumpets. Sophie, Bonnie,
Polly, and Katie carefully took hold
of the branches they'd practiced
with the day before.

Just as they were about to begin, Sophie looked up and saw the bluebird on his branch. But he wasn't blue anymore. Just like the tree, his feathers were now every color of the rainbow!

Oops, thought Sophie. But the bluebird didn't seem to mind at all. He puffed up his colorful chest proudly and began trilling his beautiful song, in harmony with the band.

118

Sophie took a deep breath. *Tail, behave!* she said in her head. She hoped the shooting-star dust would work.

Sophie's heart soared as she skipped around the tree, first this way, then that. Her tail didn't shake, so nobody sneezed. And it stayed in position, so it didn't get tangled up in the branches or trip her up. She was surrounded by a blur of lovely colors as the branches

119

of the willow tree swished to and fro. It reminded her of the beautiful shooting star and how it had drawn patterns so gracefully across the sky.

The crowd clapped and cheered as the four friends danced faster and faster around the tree. Sophie caught a glimpse of her mom and dad smiling, and her little brother laughing and clapping his paws in time.

RAINBOW BRIGHT!

And then, suddenly, it was over. All of Misty Wood cheered and clapped and drummed the ground with their paws. Sophie thought they might never stop!

At last the clapping began to die down, and the fairy animals set off to explore all the exciting things on offer at the fair. Sophie rushed over to her mom and dad to give them both a huge hug.

"We did it!" she squealed.

"You were fantastic!" Her dad grinned. "My little star!"

Sophie laughed. "Oh, but it was the *shooting* star that helped me!" she exclaimed, and gave her tail a little shake. She gasped. There was no rainbow-colored stardust left. Instead, a cloud of the usual silvery stardust shimmered in the air, then floated gently to the ground.

"It's all gone!" Sophie stared

123

at her dad. "I haven't shaken my tail since decorating the tree. I must have used it all up before the dance!" Sophie frowned. "But how did I manage to get my tail to behave if I didn't have any magical stardust left?"

Her dad patted her head with his paw. "Sometimes, all you need is to believe," he said with a smile. "You believed the stardust was going to help you—and it did.

It gave you the confidence you
needed to do the dance perfectly.
Now you can believe in yourself!"

"Wow—that really is magic!"
Sophie gasped.

"Yes, it is," said her dad. "Now
it's time you and your friends went
off to enjoy the fair. You deserve it
after all that hard work."

Sophie had been thinking so
much about the dance, she'd almost
forgotten that a whole day of

wonderful treats and surprises lay ahead.

As she fluttered off to join Katie, Bonnie, and Polly, she saw someone else flying along beside her.

"Can I come, too?" chirped the bluebird. "I want to show off my new colorful feathers."

"Of course you can!" Sophie exclaimed.

Together, Sophie and her

126

friends flew off toward the cobweb tent. The bluebird tweeted a cheerful tune as they went, and Sophie hummed along. She swished her tail happily and a trail of silver stardust shimmered in the sky behind them. What an exciting morning it had been! Today really *was* turning into the very best day of her life!

Help Sophie find the acorn
cup of delicious honey at the
center of the maze.

START

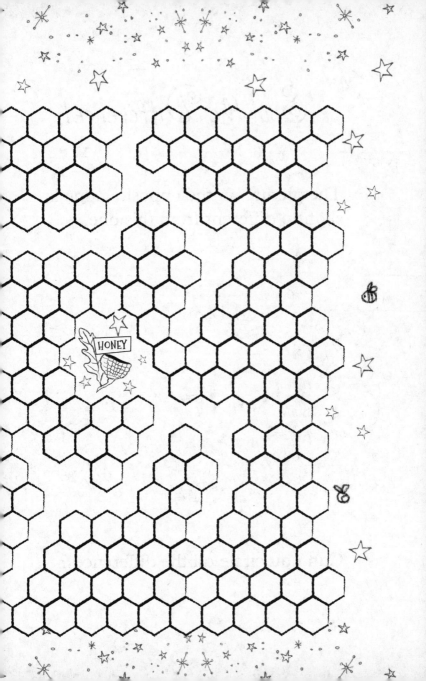

Spot the Difference!

The picture on the opposite page is slightly different from this one.

Can you circle all the differences?

Hint: There are
10 differences
in this picture!

of Misty Wood

Meet more Fairy Animal friends!